Who's Mike?

An Encounter on the Mountain

Sharon DeBord Chako

ISBN-13: 978-0692806937 (Sharon J. Chako)
ISBN-10: 0692806938
shaec99@gmail.com

DEDICATION

To my Grandchildren. You are a blessing to me. You are my inspiration. Embrace Jesus, live life out loud, and watch what happens.

CONTENT

ACKNOWLEDGMENT

To my husband, Larry. Your love for the Word of God is refreshing. You study for hours, with a passion to share what God teaches you. I have learned so much from you. You truly have a teacher's heart.

*SCRIPTURE VERSES

The life lessons in this story are all based on the truth of the Bible, the Word of God.

When you come to a chapter that has an asterisk (*) beside the heading, this means that there are supporting Scripture verses in the back of the book. Please read the verses with the chapters to get the full meaning of the life lessons.

Scripture Translations

The Scripture passages in this book are taken from the following translations:

New American Standard (NAS)
New International Version (NIV)
New Living Translation (NLT)
New King James Version (NKJV)
Amplified Bible (AMP)

THE BUS RIDE

"John, are you almost packed?" Mrs. Riley said.

John's mother was standing at the bottom of the staircase, gazing up to get a glimpse of her son's activity. The Springdale Community Church youth had worked very hard raising money to be able to take a week-long hiking trip to the Great Smoky Mountains to celebrate the end of the school year, and the beginning of summer. John was within hours of needing to be packed and ready to go.

"Yes, mom, I promise I will be packed and ready when Mr. Gibson comes by to pick me up."

John Riley was sixteen years old. He was tall and lean in stature. He was going to be a junior at Springdale High School next year. He was popular with most of his peers because of his loyalty and outgoing personality. But John's temperament could also display a cautious, easily frustrated, persistent side. He seemed to regularly question things, and could quickly spring into a debate on a variety of subjects.

Now, the only subject on John's mind was a great hiking trip as he bounced down the steps, taking two at a time, and dragging his duffle bag behind him.

"I'm all packed and ready to go," he said.

"Good, have a wonderful time, honey. Be safe and enjoy the outdoors," his mom said as she gave him a hug.

John's father entered the kitchen as they were saying their goodbyes.

"You have everything you need, son?"

"Yeah, Dad. I'm good to go."

"Ok, have a good time," Mr. Riley said as he put his arm around him and gave a squeeze.

"Take plenty of pictures – we'll be anxious to see them when you get back."

Just then Mr. Gibson pulled into the driveway, his car already packed with excited teens. Talking and laughter could be heard coming from inside the car as John quickly went out to meet them. He squeezed his duffle bag into a corner of the over packed trunk and found a place in the back seat with the other kids. It was a short distance to the church where a bus waited for them to take them on their adventure.

When Mr. Gibson arrived at Springdale Community Church, the parking lot was buzzing with all kinds of activity. There were parents saying their goodbyes and giving last minute instructions to their teens, while the kids had already mentally said good-bye and were making their break to get the best seats on the bus with their friends. Youth leaders were checking the itinerary and sounding the roll call to make sure no one was left behind. Fathers were helping to pack the bus in an organized fashion so all gear would fit. The bus filled up fast and finally, all 45 teens, youth leaders and chaperones were on board and ready to go.

As the bus traveled down the highway, the whine of the tires had a mesmerizing effect on its passengers. Several kids curled up in the seats to sleep while others played games on their tablets and phones. John sat in a seat by the window. He put his ear buds in, adjusted his phone to his favorite music and settled in for the long ride. He had a lot on his mind and wasn't in the mood for small talk.

He was beginning to feel the weight of high school. Expectations . . . so many expectations. Making the varsity team in football and basketball, maintaining an acceptable grade point average, being a good friend to his buds, attending youth group and church activities, career choices – all those career choices. The list seemed to be getting longer and longer. John was a good kid and didn't want to let anyone down – himself, his friends, and especially his parents. But right then, all he wanted to do was just forget, and kick back.

Six hours later, the bus pulled into Mountain Lion Lodge at the base of the Great Smoky Mountains. Everyone was more than happy to be out of the bus and on solid ground after the long ride from Springdale, Ohio. They made their way into the main lobby of the lodge. Immediately they were surrounded by impressive rough-hewn wood furniture and massive wood beamed ceilings. A roaring fire crackled in the large stone fireplace which took the night chill out of the air and gave a welcoming warmth to the room.

Sam Bennett, the youth leader summoned the teens to gather around for their room assignments. After assigning all of them to their rooms, he quickly gave instructions for the next morning's adventure.

"Everyone is to be up and ready to go by 7:30 and assembled in the dining room for breakfast by 8:00. After breakfast, we will board the bus and begin our journey with the first stop being the ten-mile hike up Scenic Trail. Don't stay up all night messing around. You will definitely feel the results of that tomorrow," he said with a smile.

"Ok, all of you to your rooms. See you in the morning."

A mass exodus began as kids gathered their belongings, found their roomies and headed down the hall. Soon the massive lobby, once crowded with noisy teens and piles of luggage, was once again the warm welcoming area with a crackling fire that had been there before it was invaded by the youth from Springdale.

Sharon DeBord Chako

FRIENDS

After what seemed to be a very short night, the bright sun peeked through the windows of the lodge which caused many sleepy-headed kids to know it was time to drag their bodies out of warm beds, and get ready to assemble in the dining room for breakfast. The only true motivators were good food, and the anticipation of a hike.

On his way to the dining room, John almost ran into Caleb coming out of his room.

"Hey, Caleb, how'd you sleep?" John said.

"What sleep? It seemed like I just shut my eyes, and it was morning."

Caleb was a longtime friend of John. They went to elementary school together and both had a passion for sports, especially basketball and football. He was tall in stature and physically strong. He looked older than his 17 years, and was one of the few boys in his class who needed to shave. Nobody messed with Caleb. Although, when kids took the time to get to know him, they found a kind-hearted, helpful young man, who had a good eye for evaluating a problem and the guts to solve it. You wanted him on your team.

As they turned down the hall to the main dining room, they met up with Kathryn and Abby. Kathryn and Abby were also two longtime friends of John. They both lived down the street from him. Many years of riding bikes, swimming parties and snowball fights made strong bonds between them, with a storehouse of memories, that could either be used for a good laugh or a tool for blackmail, if necessary.

Kathryn was 16 years old. She was a hardworking, self-confident girl who at times could be hard on herself. But she accomplished what she set out to do and did it well. She was a real goal setter. With her friendly nature and out-going personality, she never lacked for friends. She loved music and used it to express her heart. She wasn't a shabby athlete, either.

Abby was 15 years old with a creative eye. She could observe something ordinary like a flower pot and see how she could turn it into something beautiful – a colorful bouquet-filled work of art. Abby's personality was contagious. She had a cute smile and a funny giggle. She was helpful and giving and loved to entertain. She was a leader, and someone who knew what she wanted and how to achieve it.

The four friends entered the dining room, all talking at the same time, with excitement that built with constant conversation. Abby was giggling at John who was trying to balance a quarter on the end of his nose as he walked into the room.

"You'd better watch where you're going, John," she said. "You might just run into something and not be worth two cents." She laughed.

He smiled, constantly looking upward to keep the quarter firmly planted on the end of his nose.

"Well, that would mean I have twenty-three cents left to try it again." He laughed as the quarter fell from his nose.

"I got these new shoes just before we left Springdale," Kathryn said as she pointed her foot and turned her ankle so Caleb could get a good look at her shoe. "Actually, I got them on sale. I'm sure they will help when I'm climbing the trail," she said as she went to find a seat.

Unimpressed, Caleb said, "Yeah, I bet they will." His mind was on the food spread out on the long table in the middle of the room.

The dining room was bustling with activity. The food was hot and ready for a bunch of hungry teenagers. Everyone was ready to eat, knowing the day ahead would bring hunger pangs long before it was time to break for lunch.

Sam Bennett said, "OK, everyone, may I have your attention, please?"
He raised his hands to motion for silence and slowly conversation came to a halt. "Before we eat, let's thank the Lord for this food and ask him to guide and protect us today."

They bowed their heads as Sam prayed.

After the Amen, Sam said, "Chow down, everyone!"

The entire room came to life again as they enjoyed bacon and eggs, pancakes and syrup, bagels and cream cheese, fruit and yogurt and all the white and chocolate milk the kids could drink.

After breakfast, everyone received a sack lunch to be eaten sometime during the hike. The lunch was a treasured possession because it was known that the next time they would sit down to a warm meal was when the hike was over, and they were safely back at the lodge.

Loaded down with backpacks, they piled into the bus for the short trip to Scenic Trail.

MR. JENSEN'S GROUP

As the bus pulled into the parking lot to the entrance of the trail, Sam Bennett gave last minute instructions to the group.

"OK, now it's really important that you stick together. I will be dividing you into four groups with an adult leader. I will announce the name of each leader, and then call the names of those who are to join that group. Please exit the bus, find your leader, and group up."

One by one as their names were called, the kids exited the bus, and joined their group leader. Caleb, Kathryn, Abby and John were all part of Mr. Paul Jensen's group.

"How did this happen?" John said.

"What, that we all got into the same group?" Caleb said.

"Yes, did you pay Sam off or something? I can't believe he would put all of us in the same group."

"It's probably because he knew we were all good friends, and would work well together," Abby said. "That's not a bad thing, you know."

Mr. Jensen was a local attorney in Springdale. He was a friendly man who taught Sunday School for the seventh and eighth grade kids at Springdale Community Church. The kids were comfortable being around him, and were quite excited when they discovered he was going to be their leader.

"Wow, I'm so glad we're in Mr. Jensen's group," Abby whispered to Kathryn. "He's pretty cool."

"I know. I agree."

In addition to John and his friends, Silas, Kelly and Mindy finished out Mr. Jensen's group. Silas, who was Mr. Jensen's son, was 15 years old and smarter than his years showed. An avid reader, he seemed to know something about everything. If anyone wanted to know something, Silas was the one to ask. He was one of the few kids on the trip that wasn't as enthusiastic about climbing mountains as some others. He would rather have stayed behind, and read a good book. But friendships make strong ties at this age, and he wanted to be with his friends. The kids liked Silas, not just for the information he could provide but because he was understanding and compassionate, and his easy-going nature made him pleasant to be around.

Kelly was 18 years old and in her last year of high school. College was looking exceptionally good to her as she was ready to spread her wings and fly. She was a leader out and out. She could evaluate any given situation and come up with a solid strategy to get the results she wanted. She had no problem taking leadership, and did so in a supportive and kind way, although at times she could get frustrated with quitters and whiners. She was creative and hard-working with a stellar imagination. And on top of all that, she was very pretty.

Mindy was a character. Her out-going and friendly personality drew many friends, and Mindy had lots of them. Everyone seemed to know Mindy. She loved to have fun. Life was a party to her and if anyone wanted a party, she was the one to go to. She loved the arts and music, and at 14 years of age, she could get up on her soapbox and recite passages from a Shakespeare play that would make any avid Broadway actor stand up and take notice. She was *very* dramatic which at times made her friends comment, "Oh, pa-a-lezze!!" But her smile was infectious, and her eyes danced with joy.

Mr. Jensen gathered his group together and said, "It's ten o'clock in the morning and time to get hiking. Does everyone have all the required supplies? You should be carrying an extra pair of dry socks, a windbreaker, some protein snacks, a bottle of water, and of course your sack lunch." All of them opened their backpacks to do a double check, and nodded that all was packed.

"Believe me, you will want them," he said. "Also, you can take your cell phones along, but there will be many places you won't be able to use them because of the lack of connecting with a phone tower. Remember, we are out here to enjoy nature, and each other. The cell phones are only to be used for emergencies."

After all last-minute instructions were given, Mr. Jensen motioned to his group, and they walked to the path that started their journey up Scenic Trail.

One by one the other groups organized and received their instructions by each of their leaders, and by 10:15 the entire youth group was on its way. The chatter was continuous as they followed their leaders, single file, up the path.

Sam Bennett, who was the leader of one of the other groups, explained to everyone before the hike started to look for several forks in the path. Each fork would have a post beside it in a certain color. To make the hike more fun, he would assign each group a color. Each group was to split off into the path that had its color. At the end of the ten-mile hike, the paths would merge together again, coming to an end at the back of the Mountain Lion Lodge. The purpose was to be able to share the individual group's experience with everyone once the hike was over.

He said, "Each path has its own interesting twists and turns, and it will be exciting to hear how each group navigated the journey."

He announced the colors for each group. Mr. Jensen's group had the color, blue.

It wasn't long into the hike when the first fork came into view. It had a green post beside it and happily one group was on its way. Everyone waved goodbye.

Caleb shouted, "Watch out for bears."

"Yeah, don't trip over any snakes," Silas said, as they laughed at the surprised look on several of the girls' faces.

The remaining groups picked up the pace as the path started to incline. As they got to the top of a hill, there were two forks in the road. One went to the left and the other to the right with the main trail straight ahead. The fork to the left had a yellow post and the fork to the right had a red post. Each group with its assigned colors headed in the direction of its post's color. They waved goodbye as they made their way down the paths and out of sight.

"Well, I don't see a colored post for the path ahead," Mr. Jensen said, "But since we are the last group and all the others have found their paths, it seems logical that the path straight ahead is ours."

"Yes, as a matter of fact it is," said Silas. "I just walked over here to the edge of the path and uncovered the blue post marker that has been covered up by this vine." He raised up his arm with a handful of a large green vine that stretched the length of is body.

"If each path is supposed to have a marker, then our path is no exception," he added. "I knew it had to be here somewhere."

"Way to go. Silas. We can always depend on you," Mindy said as she smiled and gave him a big slap on the back.

"OK, guys, let's get headed up this mountain," Mr. Jensen said. Everyone eagerly followed in step behind their leader.

THE FALL

It seemed natural for the boys to fall in line behind Mr. Jensen, followed closely by the girls with their non-stop conversation. The trail was wide and could easily accommodate two hikers side by side, which made talking much easier. On the right side of the trail was the mountain which displayed huge boulders and jagged moss-covered rock that protruded high above their heads. Sometimes the boulders were so big they would bulge out into the trail.

Black stains could be seen on the boulders which showed proof of the many hikers who had been there before and placed their hands on the rock as they walked by. On the left side of the trail was a deep ravine that dropped off several hundred feet. It was covered with green vegetation and beautiful wildflowers. Smaller, less dominating rocks made their presence known by peeking out from the vegetation below.

Tall mighty trees reached for the sky while smaller tender saplings fought for sunlight. There were trees that had sprouted up so close to the trail that roots extended across the path. Mr. Jensen alerted everyone to be careful and keep an eye out for the roots.

"Yeah, they can be a real trip," Caleb said as the girls giggled.

"I think the wildflowers are so beautiful down in the ravine," Abby said, "I would love to get down there and pick a bouquet."

"I don't think that will happen," Silas said. "I read that a horse fell down a sixty-foot ravine, and the rescue took an extensive operation including a hoist to get it out. This ravine is much steeper," he said as he pointed down the slope. "You might get down there to pick a few flowers, but I don't think you would be able to make it back up by yourself."

"She's not a horse, you know," Mindy said.

"Yeah, and that's not a sixty-foot ravine either. It's probably more like a couple hundred feet."

"Maybe we'll find some flowers along the trail up ahead," Mindy said as she passed Silas leaving him standing in the middle of the path by himself.

The blue trail group continued down the footpath taking in all the sights and sounds of the woods covered mountain. By this time the dynamics of the group had changed. Mindy and Abby had gone ahead of the boys to talk with Mr. Jensen, while John, Silas and Caleb hung back to walk with the other girls.

John was walking with Kelly. A spirited conversation was taking place about upcoming summer activities.

"I'm going to have as much fun as I can this summer," John said. "I've been working very hard this school year to get my grades up, and I'm ready for a nice long break."

Kelly looked at him and smiled. "I'm going to look for a summer job to get ready to go to college. I plan to get serious about finding something after we get back from this trip. Every penny helps you know," she said as she rolled her eyes and sighed.

"Yep, you got that right," he said as he began to trot up the trail shooting imaginary hoops with his right hand.

He turned and walked backwards, making dramatic antics, imitating an NBA player. He yelled to the kids behind him, "Watch this – there's three seconds left and the score is tied . . . he runs, he jumps, he shoots!"

He jumped in the air demonstrating a perfect jump shot. But as he came down, his foot hit one of the large roots that had grown across the path, causing him to lose his balance.

He tried his best to keep from falling. But his momentum pushed him to the ravine side of the mountain. As he struggled to get his footing, his other foot slid toward the side of the path where loose stones and dirt grabbed his foot and pulled him in.

"John, look out!" Kathryn screamed.

"Dude, be careful!" Caleb shouted.

Kelly ran to try to grab him, but it was too late. "No! No!" she cried.

Much to the astonishment of all who were watching, John fell on the edge of the path which gave way to the ravine below. His body tumbled and tumbled down the hill, colliding with rocks, bumping into trees and getting tangled in the thick vegetation.

*WHY ARE YOU HERE?

"John . . . John!" John opened his eyes to a blurry vision of a man standing over him. As he blinked several times, trying to focus, the man bent down and offered him his hand.

"Hi, my name is Mike, let me help you up."

"Who?"

"Mike. I'm a guide on this mountain trail. You looked like you needed some help. I'm here to help."

"Where's Mr. Jensen?

"His phone rang. Something came up and he needed to leave. So, that's why I'm here."

"Oh," John said as he tried to shake off the fog in his mind.

Mike was average in height and build with dark hair and piercing eyes. He was rugged looking, an obvious outdoorsman. But beyond his woodsy appearance, he displayed a warm caring disposition. John gripped the man's hand, and, much to his amazement, the next thing he knew, they were out of the ravine and back on the trail. Maybe it was his dizziness that kept him from being too concerned about details. He was just glad to be on solid ground.

When he saw the surprised look on the faces of his friends, he said, "Hey, I'm cool and this is Mike."

"Who's Mike?" Caleb said.

"Yeah, who is he? Kelly added.

"He's going to be our guide because Mr. Jensen was called away."

"I hope there's not an emergency with one of the other groups," Mindy said.

"It's really a good thing he was able to use his cell phone. There are so many places up here where it doesn't work," Abby said.

"Hey, don't forget, my dad is an attorney. He's always getting called away for something," Silas added.

"Well, I'm sure we will hear all the details later. But right now, why are we waiting around here? We're burning daylight. Let's hike," John said.

Mike motioned to the other kids to join them as they continued up the trail. The beautiful sights and sounds of the forest were enchanting. The girls talked as they walked along. They were comfortable with Mike as their trail leader. He seemed to fit in so well.

The trail began a steep incline and the tree roots that spread inconsistently across the path were once again causing havoc to its travelers. Silas was heard huffing and puffing in the back of the group.

"Hey, Si," Mindy said. "Is that you or is that your mom's vacuum cleaner I hear?" Everyone laughed.

"Sounds like your sucking a lot of air, Silas," Caleb said.

"Well, you do know that the higher you go, the air in the atmosphere gets thinner, don't you?"

"So, do you know the percentage of air in the atmosphere right now?" Kelly asked.

"Well, no, but I would be able to find out if I were able to use my cell phone," Silas said.

"By the way, sorry to change the subject," Mike said. "But I have a question for all of you. Why are you here?"

Mindy answered, "I wanted to come on this outing to be with my friends."

"Yeah, me too," Abby said, "And besides, I just love nature, with all the birds and the flowers and the trees. It's beautiful. It makes me want to stop and paint a picture."

Kelly said, "I just think it's healthy to get out and exercise. I like to push myself to experience new challenges."

"That's why I came, and of course, to hang out with my friends too," Kathryn said.

"It's an adventure, something different," John said, "It beats staying at home and doing chores."

"No, that's not exactly what I meant by asking 'why are you here?'" Mike said.

"Let's take a short rest. We'll stop at this little cove ahead and catch our breath, and I will explain what I meant."

They reached the cove and found nice smooth boulders at the base of the mountainside that had been carved out by nature. They looked like good seats for tired hikers. It was refreshing to sit a while. Some of the kids were taking off their shoes and rubbing their feet, while others were shedding jackets and sweaters.

"When I asked you, 'why are you here?' what I meant was, why are you alive? Why do you exist? What's your purpose for living? Do you know?" Mike said.

Silence swept across them as they stopped what they were doing and stared motionless at him. It was obvious they had not been thinking about his question in that way at all.

Finally, Kelly said, "Well, I believe we are here on this earth to honor God with our lives and to love other people."

"Yeah, that's good," the others agreed.

"I think we should also be honest and hardworking and good examples of how the Bible teaches us to live," Silas said.

Mike stood up and faced the group. He slowly paced back and forth in front of the kids.

"Those are some good comments, and I appreciate your honesty in sharing them, but did you know God has a special plan and a purpose for each one of you? He has a reason for you being here on this earth, at this time, as well as being on this hike. And He wants each one of you to know what that purpose is. Let me share with you God's purpose for why you are here. I call it God's divine design for mankind. Where in the Bible did the story of mankind begin?"

Silas immediately jumped up and said, "Oh, I know, Genesis. And Genesis means beginnings."

"You're right, Silas. God created mankind in His own image. What do you think that means? Have any of you ever seen God? Do you know what God looks like?"

They all shook their heads and mumbled "no."

"When God created the first man and woman, Adam and Eve, He designed them so that He could live in them. Genesis says that God breathed into the nostrils of man, and he became a living soul. God breathed *His* life into Adam. This breath of life was more than just physical life." Mike stopped pacing and stood directly in front of the group, looking squarely into their eyes.

"God gave to the first man and woman the gift of sharing *His* very life. And, the ability for sharing His life would come from Him. How they behaved would show God's character, that is, how He thinks, and how He acts, because He was the source that would make it happen. Let me give you an example of what I mean."

He ran his hands through his hair and then stretched out his arms in front of him, giving an all-inclusive gesture towards the kids. "You all know that a car runs on gas, right?" They all shook their heads in agreement.

"Even though the car has the capacity, or shall we say the gas tank, to make it function, it has no ability to fill itself up and function in the way it was designed to function. Therefore, it needs an outside source to fill it with the exact fuel designed for it. Likewise, God created people to function and fulfill their roles in dependence on Him – the source for filling – so that the very presence of His life – the fuel – might enable them to live out His likeness and character – the function or purpose. In other words, He is the one who fills: He's the outside source, and He's also the exact fuel needed, because He fills people up with Himself. As a person trusts or depends on Him, He is the motivator that puts His life and character into action. And do you know what is cool about all of this?"

Kathryn said, "No, what is it?"

Mike came over to sit down on the stone bench beside Caleb. He leaned in toward the rest of the group.

"God didn't want people to be like robots. He designed people to have a relationship with Him, to know and experience Him. It's an active relationship where He loves them and they love him back. And out of their love for Him, they depend on Him and obey Him so that His life can be lived out through them. The intent was, when one would observe a person in action, one would be able to see what God is like. So, a person, by what he says, he does, and he is, was designed to show what God is like. What an awesome plan! God's purpose for creating people was, number one, to have a relationship with his people, and, number two, that his people would show what He is like. It's God's divine design for mankind."

The kids seemed to be deep in thought. This was not what they were expecting to hear. Although it was unexpected, Mike's words started some serious thinking.

*THE GARDEN

Mike got up from the bench he was sitting on and motioned to the group, "Come on, I think we've rested enough. I think we're good to go."

They put on their shoes and jackets, grabbed backpacks, and moved out of the cove and back on the trail. They hadn't gone very far before John said, "Hey Mike, I've got a question."

"What's that?"

"If God's purpose was to have a relationship with us, and for us to show what He is like, then obviously, something happened along the way because we don't have to look very far to see that many people, by the way they act, do not show what God is like. I know I don't always act in ways that show what God is like. And we all know people who have no relationship with God at all."

"Now that's weird because I was just thinking the same thing before you even brought it up," Abby said as she came alongside John.

Mike turned back to face them, carefully walking backwards and said, "I didn't say that was the end of the story. Actually, it's just the beginning." And with a quick turn he headed up the trail again.

"Of course," Silas said, raising his hands above his head, "I told you Genesis means beginnings!"

"Ok, Si, we got it" Mindy said as she gave him a smile.

As they walked along, Mike began to speak again.

"John brought up a good thought. We don't see everybody showing what God is like. You're right. There was a problem that entered the scene. Does anybody know what happened in Genesis in the Garden of Eden after God created Adam and Eve?"

"Yeah, I do," Kelly said. "Sin entered into the scene and that changed everything. God told Adam and Eve that they were to take care of the garden. They had freedom in the garden to eat from any tree in there except from one of the trees in the middle of the garden. It was called *the tree of the knowledge of good and evil.* God said that if they would eat from that tree they would die."

"That's right," Silas said.

"And one day when they were in the garden, Satan showed up in the form of a serpent. Don't know exactly what that looked like, but they didn't seem to be afraid of him. You'd think Eve would have freaked out, just like my sister would, if a snake, or a serpent would even come close to her. But the woman is having a conversation with him. F r e a k y! Talking snakes! I guess things were different then."

Silas picked up his pace and came along side Kelly as they walked.

"Anyway, he says, listen woman, you're not going to die. God's holding out on you. He knows that when you eat the fruit on that tree you will be like Him, knowing good and evil. 'Humm' she thinks. Who wouldn't want that? So, she sashays up to the tree, taking in the aroma and beauty of the fruit on it. The girlfriend reaches out and takes a piece of the forbidden fruit and eats it! And here's my man Adam, just hangin' out watching all this, knowing what God had told them about eating from the tree, but not doing anything to stop his wife."

He leans in toward Kelly, "Here's the real kicker. Eve skips over to her man and says 'here you go, Sweetie, take a bite. It's soooo good.'"

He yells, "He takes a big bite! Did he bump his head? I guess misery loves company because that's just what they got – misery."

"Wow, Silas. I didn't know you had that in you. What a story teller," Kelly said.

Abby said, "I loved it Silas."

*DEAD OR ALIVE

They walked along in silence for quite some time, trying to decide just what they thought of Mike's question. Suddenly an unusual sound broke the silence. Kathryn turned and looked at John, what was that?" she said. They began to laugh.

"That's my stomach growling. I'm here to tell you, I'm hungry!" Silas said.

John cupped his hands around his mouth and yelled to Mike, "We have a hungry one here, Mike. I think if we don't stop for lunch soon, Silas may just fade away."

"Well, actually, I'm kind of hungry myself," Kathryn whispered.

"Yeah, me too," John said.

Mike motioned for the group to huddle up so they could decide where they were going to stop to eat the lunches they had packed.

"It's about time we stop for lunch. Besides, if you don't eat the sandwiches soon, they may start to spoil on you. We wouldn't want that to happen, would we?"

"Absolutely not!" Silas said.

"Let's go up here around the bend in the trail to the mountain ridge. It levels off, and there are some real nice grassy areas where we can stop for lunch," Mike said.

Everyone agreed and happily continued to the grassy plateau. Once seated on the ground with lunches unpacked, the food disappeared at the speed of light.

Mike said, “We talked a little earlier about what happened to Adam and Eve in the Garden of Eden. We got some very colorful details about the events, thanks to Silas.”

Silas took a bow, bending at the waist, almost touching his face to his knees since he was seated Indian-style on the ground.

“But I think we need to look at the story with more detail. Eve was tricked but Adam knew what his wife did was wrong, and through a chosen act of disobedience he joined her. God held Adam responsible for his actions. Now here’s the bag of lies Satan sold to Adam and Eve: a person could be the source of his own activity apart from God, meaning they were in control of their lives instead of Him. Remember the story I told you about the car? A car doesn’t work well on its own. Neither do people. And because they listened to Satan, they acted in direct disobedience to God, deciding on their own what they would do.”

Mindy said, “It sounds like they didn’t act out of love for God, and they didn’t want to trust him for their lives. Obeying him wasn’t a big deal.”

“Maybe they decided that instead of loving and protecting them, He was being too strict, holding something back from them. Or, since they were His children, maybe they thought He’d cut them a break this time, and let it slide,” Caleb said.

Mike got up from the ground and brushed the grass from his pants, “They determined in their minds that, ‘we don’t need God, we can handle this on our own.’ Now, God said that if you eat from the *tree of the knowledge of good and evil*, you will die. Did God get soft? Did He back down? Did He change his mind? Did they die?”

Abby spoke up and said, “Well, no, they didn’t just fall over dead right in the middle of the garden. God met up with them later.”

“Yeah, that would be one tough meeting. That’s probably why they were hiding from God. They already knew they did wrong, feelin’ guilty,” Kelly said.

"Like when you're in trouble with your parents and you stay up in your bedroom only to have them call you downstairs for a conference. Awkward!" John said as he rolled his eyes.

Mike walked around the group sitting in a circle. His hands were clasp together behind him and he chose his words very carefully, not wanting any misunderstanding in what he was about to say.

"Yes, God did meet up with them later and that meeting had huge, life changing results, not only for them, but for the rest of mankind, including you and me. Here's the tragedy. Because Adam and Eve acted in independence from God instead of dependence on Him, and in that act disobeyed Him, they sinned. Sin is missing the mark, or God's standard for life with Him. Consequently, the spiritual life of God was taken from them. The life that He had originally breathed into Adam, God's life, was removed.

"This not only started the cycle of aging and physical death but unfortunately resulted in spiritual death and separation from God. And that's how every person who has ever lived starts out. We are all born into the family of Adam. We are all born in sin, separated from the life of God. There is nothing we can do on our own to change that. We can't be good enough. We can't do enough. We can't give enough to change who we are.

"Is God being mean? Is He hardhearted, a bully? No, just the opposite. If He let sin slide, He would no longer be God. He would no longer be able to rescue us from ourselves, and from evil. He is righteous and holy and His standard for life is holy. He is unchangeable, and His word is unchangeable and believe me, we wouldn't want it any other way."

He stopped and looked directly at the kids seated on the ground.

"While all this may sound tragic, and it is, there's good news. This is not the end of the story. God didn't want to leave us in that condition. He loved what He had created. But He knew for us to have a relationship with Him, we would need His life restored to us, and we would need our sins forgiven. Something we could not do on our own.

"So, God sent His son, Jesus Christ to this earth to pay the penalty for our sin because His perfect sinless life was the only one

God would accept as payment for our sin. When we receive God's gift of Jesus Christ, as His way to restore life into our dead spirits, we become alive unto God, having His life, and likeness restored to us.

"Jesus also paid the sin debt that separated us from God. When God's life is restored to us, and our sins forgiven, we are partners with Him, sharing His life. We become his sons and daughters. We are born into the family of God."

At this point, Mike sat down again in the circle of kids. His eyes slowly moved from one person to the next as he continued, "I guess at this point I need to pose a question to all of you because it's a matter of life or death to everyone here. It's that important. The question is, are you dead or are you alive? Is the life of God still removed from you – or have you come alive to God? Have your sins been forgiven by receiving His gift of Jesus?"

There was a long pause of silence as one by one they thought through his question to them. Then, "I'm alive" echoed throughout the circle as they confirmed to Mike that God's life had been restored to them, and they had been forgiven.

"Well, then let's move on," Mike said.

They gathered up their belongings and continued to hike.

THE BEARS

The next stretch of the journey was more pleasant since the trail became wide and flat. The tree roots that were so treacherous had disappeared. The boys joked with each other and teased the girls. Unimpressed with their antics, Kelly and Kathryn decided to join Mike at the front of the pack.

"Do you guys know how annoying you can be?" Kathryn said as she passed the boys.

"Of course we do," John said, "That's just part of who we are. Isn't that awesome?"

Kelly laughed as she passed John, "You guys are such nerds!"

No one noticed that Abby and Mindy trailed behind. They became fascinated with the beautiful yellow, pink and violet wildflowers mingled with clover and grass that spread across the meadow-like plateau. Bees were busy going from clover to flower unafraid and unimpressed by the presence of travelers.

Abby was fully engaged in picking bouquets and pressing her nose on each flower to smell its fragrance. Neither girl realized how long they had been enjoying the meadow until Mindy abruptly interrupted Abby.

"Hey, we'd better get a move on. I've lost sight of everybody."

With Abby jolted out of her meadow experience, and the urgency of Mindy's voice, both girls sprinted to catch up with the others, but by then they were nowhere to be seen.

"Ok, no need to panic here," Mindy said. "Just because we can't see them doesn't mean we can't find them. After all, where can they go? They must be on the path. Let's just pick up the pace and we should catch up with them in no time."

"I hope you're right," Abby said as she started walking up the trail as fast as she could.

In their excitement, they failed to see a female black bear with two cubs that had made their way into the meadow. The bears seemed to be indifferent to the girl's presence. They were totally absorbed in hunting berries and other choice delicacies as they lumbered along.

Suddenly Abby spotted the big mother bear. "Oh no," she said as she grabbed Mindy's arm and squeezed it. "Look! Over there, see the bears? What do we do now?"

The bears had positioned themselves between the girls and the path they needed to take to join the others.

"I don't know. I'm afraid. What if they get on the trail and start heading this way? Where should we go?" Mindy said as she started to cry.

"Maybe we can just go back into the meadow where the grass is taller and stay down and hide until they leave," Abby said. "It looks like all they are interested in is finding food."

"Yeah, and they can find us and eat us for lunch!" Mindy said sarcastically.

Just then the bears made their way onto the trail, still hunting for food. They totally blocked the girls from getting to the rest of the kids. The girls turned back toward the path they had come from and started to run away when they heard Mike's voice.

"Girls! Girls!" He spoke with a firm commanding voice. "Stop, do not run!"

Mindy and Abby stopped in their tracks and turned back to see Mike slowly walking toward the bears on the path. He waved his hands in the air to get their attention while staying a good distance away. The mother bear stood up on her hind legs and looked directly at him for a moment. Everyone stood motionless for what seemed a lifetime. Then she slowly returned to her hunt for food and lumbered across the path and into the meadow below. Her two cubs eagerly followed her unaffected by the human activity.

When the bears were a good distance away, Mike motioned for the girls to come his way. They sprinted towards him, squealing with joy.

He put his finger to his mouth . . . "Shhhhhh."

He eyed the mother bear to make sure she hadn't decided to turn back, and then put his arms around both girls and led them back to the others.

"Boy, we are glad to see you," Abby said.

"Yeah, I just saw my life flash before my eyes, and it was a short one too," Mindy said.

Kathryn came up to them, "Well, we're all glad you're safe. From now on, stick a little closer to us. We didn't even notice you were gone."

"We'll stick like glue," Abby said.

CALEB

After an hour of hiking, the trail started to narrow, the foliage thickened beside the path and tall trees spread their leafy branches hiding the sun. Once again, the ravine appeared on the left side of the trail while the mountain hugged the right. Strong tree roots made their way across the path again and by now everyone was very familiar with the hazard and carefully chose each step. Caleb walked by himself, seemingly deep in thought. Everyone noticed, but no one said anything to him. John and Silas were deep in conversation about the next new game app for their smart phones. The girls eagerly chatted behind them as Abby and Mindy relived the bear incident in dramatic fashion.

Slowly Caleb made his way to the front of the line where Mike was leading the group. He walked beside Mike, not saying anything for a while. Then he spoke in a soft quiet voice.

"I've been doing a lot of thinking, Mike."

"About what?"

"About all this stuff with Adam and Eve. I've heard the story since I was a child, but I didn't *really* know the story. When you shared about their choice to disobey God, I never realized how bad their choice was, and how the result of their choice affects me.

You said that everyone that has ever been born starts out in the family of Adam. We start out separated from God and spiritually dead in sin. You know, that explains a lot. I've always felt that there must be more to this life. I just didn't know what."

"You went on to say that unless we receive the gift of God's son Jesus, to pay the sin debt that we got from Adam, we remain separated from God. His life has not been restored in us."

They picked up the pace as they walked along.

"The last thing you said to us was, 'are you dead or are you alive?' Mike, I realized I was dead. I knew I was empty inside, but didn't know what to do about it. I tried to fill the emptiness with all kinds of things like sports, video games, entertainment. Those things filled up my time, but never took away the emptiness.

"I really didn't like going home and spending time in my bedroom where it was quiet, and I had time to think. I didn't want to think, so I either played sports or listened to music, or played games on the computer or on my phone. I needed to keep busy so I didn't have to think about my loneliness.

"I also thought going to church regularly and hanging out with kids from the youth group might help. It did supply me with a great group of friends, but did nothing about the emptiness inside. All these things were temporary fixes that didn't last. And so, I've had to come to grips with the fact that I was dead, spiritually dead. I had never been taken from the family of Adam and placed into God's family. I had never received forgiveness for my sins.

"So, as we walked along in the meadow back there I prayed to God and asked Him to give me Jesus. I said that I believe You sent Him to pay for my sin. But most of all, I want Your life alive in me. I want to know You, *really* know You."

Caleb stopped and grabbed Mike's arm and turned to look him straight in the face. Tears welled up in his eyes as his chin quivered and he said, "Mike, I'm alive!"

A big broad smile swept across his face. "The emptiness is gone, and it feels like a big weight has been lifted from me."

Mike's face broke into a big smile, and he gave Caleb a big bear hug.

"I'm so happy for you."

The rest of the group sensed they were deep in conversation. They knew Caleb had not been himself for quite some time, so they kept their distance out of respect.

Mike motioned for the group to join them and said, "Caleb has something he would like to share with you."

"Yes, I do," Caleb said. "I just want you all to know that when I started the hike up this mountain I belonged to one family, the family of Adam. But I'm going to finish this hike born into another family, God's family. I started out dead, but I'm going to finish alive!"

They all started cheering. John and Silas came up and shook his hand.

John said, "Welcome to the family, man."

"Yeah, that's great," Silas said with a smile.

One by one, the girls came up to Caleb with tears in their eyes and gave him a hug.

"Whew! What a day," Mike said as he raised his head and looked to the sky. "We have quite a bit of trail left, so let's get moving."

They adjusted their backpacks and continued.

"There could be some interesting twists and turns ahead," Mike said as he looked back to make sure everyone was following him. No one was real clear on what he meant, and it didn't seem to bother them . . . yet.

*FOG . . . FOG . . . FOG

The trail began rising with sharp turns that took more and more energy to keep a good pace. Everyone noticed a dense fog starting to settle upon the trees. It slowly descended on the trail ahead.

"Mike," John yelled, "It looks like it could get pretty bad up there."

"Yes, I know, it tends to do that sometimes. We'll be fine if we stay on the trail."

"That's if we can see the trail," Mindy said.

Kelly took her position beside Mike as they walked along. She finally spoke after a few minutes of silence.

"When you told us about God giving His son Jesus to us, His life was also payment for our sins, right?"

"Yes, not only was it to restore His life in us but to take care of another problem. You see, there was a two-fold problem of sin and sins: what I am and what I do. Sin is an attitude of independence from God and sins are the things done because of this inner attitude.

"Sin is the root. Sins are the fruit. We all begin life with this two-fold problem. We're not sinners because we commit sins.

We commit sins because we are sinners by nature. Therefore, because we have this two-fold problem of sin and sins, we need forgiveness for what we have done, and we need freedom from who we are, sinners.

"Jesus freely gave his life by shedding his blood and dying on a cross to pay our sin debt. He took our place and paid the price for our sins and rescued us from our lives as sinners. His life was the only payment God would accept because his life was the only sinless life ever lived. He completely satisfied the just demands of a Holy God. And three days later, God raised him from the dead to show He accepted Jesus' sacrifice for us. You remember, we've already talked about this, right?"

"Yes, I remember," Kelly said. "Thanks, Mike. I'm starting to understand this. It makes a lot of sense, and I'm starting to connect the dots on some things I never understood before."

The longer they hiked, the fog became so dense until it was almost impossible to see 20 feet ahead. Not knowing what the trail was like, several kids hesitated going any farther.

Mike gathered the group together. "Listen," he said, "I've taken this trail more times than you can imagine. I know it well. The fog is a hazard, I know, but it's not a journey stopper. Now, here are the choices you have: you can push through the fog and continue the trail, or you can decide to stop here and turn around and go back the way you came. The choice is yours."

He waited a few minutes and then added, "Oh, and by the way, I'm pushing through the fog and going on. If you decide to turn back, you'll be on your own. So, who's going with me?" And with that, he turned and started walking.

"I'm in," said Silas.

"Me, too," said Kelly.

Mindy and Abby said nothing but ran past all of them to catch up with Mike. They were determined not to be left behind this time.

As the fog grew more intense, the group stuck close together, hanging on to each other as they were instructed by their guide.

"I don't know why I came on this trip," John said. "This is not what I thought it would be like. It's been hard, tiring, and even scary at times. I thought this was supposed to be fun."

"Yeah, I'm kind of afraid," Kathryn said. "When I can't see what's ahead, it freaks me out."

"Things don't always turn out the way you think they are supposed to, John," Kelly said.

"And, fear is a natural response to the unknown," Silas added.

As they walked along, Caleb stumbled on a large root that had grown across the path. He was thrust forward and ran directly into Silas who fell to the ground.

"Sorry, dude," Caleb said as he bent down to help Silas to his feet.

"No problem," Silas said. "I just tripped over that same root myself."

"I just had a tree branch slap me in the face," John said. I didn't see that coming either."

"Mike?" Mindy said. "Are you there? I can't see you at all. This fog all around me looks like monsters and ghosts coming at me. They just roll and twist and form ugly faces that seem to come at me, and then everything disappears only to have more roll in again. When will this be over? I really want to quit."

"We're almost through the fog. Just a little farther," Mike said.

"Just because you can't see the trail ahead or you can't see me doesn't mean I'm not here leading you. Is everyone still holding on to the person in front of you?"

A resounding "yes" could be heard.

"Ok, let's keep going."

Mike's words were encouraging and the group pressed on. It wasn't long before the fog started to thin out. It was easier to see the path ahead and the anxiety everyone experienced started to vanish. A nice bend in the trail came at just the most welcomed time. Once past the bend, it was clear. The fog had lifted and the mist was gone.

"Wow, glad that's over," Silas said with a big sigh.

**DON'T BLOW IT OFF*

A foliage covered ravine once again appeared to the left of them with mighty oak trees reaching the sky. The mountain to the right rose even higher with its jagged moss-covered rock and tree saplings making impressive appearances here and there. Mike directed the hikers to a small opening between the trail and the side of the mountain. They sat down on the ground and on large rocks while they caught their breath.

"I'm proud of you guys. No one quit. Everyone pressed on. That's huge." He unzipped his jacket, took it off and tossed it on a large tree branch next to the trail.

Wiping the sweat from his forehead, he said, "There's something we talked about earlier that I would like to put into the fog event we just experienced. Remember we talked about God's divine design for mankind?" They shook their heads in agreement.

He continued, "God's original purpose for creating people was, that in relationship with Him, they could show what God is like.

"Have there been times in your life when it would be hard for others to see what God is like? Has it been hard to please God in the way you would like? Do you even know what that kind of life is supposed to look like?"

Kelly said, "I know for myself it has always been a challenge to follow Jesus in the way that I know is pleasing to Him. I read the Bible which tells me how to live, but putting that into practice is something else." The others agreed.

"I want you to remember the fog we just experienced," Mike said. "You couldn't see where you were going. You didn't like the fact that you weren't in control. Some of you were afraid. Others became discouraged. And a few of you would have turned around and gone back the way you came, satisfied to stay with what you had already experienced on this hike, rather than pushing through the fog and going on to finish the trail.

"This is much like the fog that blows into our lives as Christians. It can take on different appearances, much like what Mindy thought she saw, as we walked along. One problem the fog brings to us is what I like to call self-centeredness. It is at the root of who we are. We will do whatever it takes to protect what we like and want. We like things to go our way. One of the greatest tragedies of sin, is selfishness. It attacks every area of life. It flows over into our relationship with Jesus, in that we have this idea of what our relationship with Him should be like. We do all the right things, say the right things and hide all the other stuff. . . *as if He doesn't know*. And we think, God certainly should be pleased with us, at least, as pleased as we are of ourselves. Life should go well, right?

"But, then, we experience bumps in the road. Things don't go like we planned. Friendships don't work out. Disappointments occur. So, our relationship with Jesus falls flat. Tragedy happens, and we lose hope or get angry and say, 'I'm starting to question the value of this relationship. What's the point?' Or we say, 'I guess I need to try harder, or I need to be more self-controlled.' But what if things don't change, or perhaps, get worse? What do we say then? 'What's the use of trying? The harder I try, the harder it gets.' It's all about I . . .I . . .I.

"Then, the fog blows the culture or world values at us. It suggests how we are to dress, how we entertain ourselves, how we pick our friends, where we go, and especially what we believe. It shapes our thoughts and drives our actions. We can allow world values to influence us so much to the point where our actions and attitudes aren't any different from those around us who have no relationship with Jesus at all. Do we know the difference? Can we see the difference?

"Last, but not least, the fog blows Satan at us. If we truly belong to the family of God, there is nothing Satan can do to change that. So, the next best thing he can do is to make our lives unproductive and ineffective for God. I want you to think about this. Satan is a liar. He thrives on imposing delusion and discouragement on us. He is the master accuser. He loves to bring up past failures and sins. He doesn't present himself to us like we see in pictures; as an ugly red form with horns and a pitchfork. He's also a radiant light that can tempt us, and draw us into his control. He wants to get us to think we are missing out on something exciting. He uses distractions, in the form of worldly pleasure, and busyness to keep us from experiencing the fullness, and pleasure of a day to day relationship with the God of the universe.

"So, the fog in the life of a Christian is significant. It cannot, well, to use a fitting term, be blown off. Because if we don't recognize the fog in our lives, we will settle to live an average Christian existence, going through the traditional experiences and roles of church life and being 'ok' with that. We might decide to be content to stay on the safe side of the mountain, on the trail we know, not pushing through the fog to experience the fullness of God in our lives."

He walked around them, carefully looking at each hiker.

"Maybe you're satisfied with what you know. Maybe you'd rather play it safe. Stepping out and letting go? Trusting God every day for all things big and little, instead of depending on self? Seeking Him in deeper ways? Resisting the pull of world values? Living in victory over Satan and his power? Having an active close ongoing friendship with Jesus? Well, that's another story.

"So, once again, I pose a question to all of you: which side of the fog are you going to stay on? What kind of Christian life do you want to live here, and now?"

He paused, then said, "You don't have to actually answer me. I just want you to think about it."

And with that, he grabbed his jacket and started walking up the trail as he motioned for them to join him.

THE WATERFALLS

One by one the hikers walked in single file behind Mike. The sun was beginning to peak through the trees toward the west as shadows lengthened which indicated that it was mid-afternoon. A loud continuous rumble could be heard in the distance. It seemed to get louder as they walked.

Finally, Caleb shouted, "What's that noise?"

"Yeah, what is it? It's so loud it's beginning to hurt my ears," Abby said.

"We're coming up on a difficult part of the trail," Mike said as he turned his head to answer.

"It's not impossible, but it might be a challenge. Keep one thing in mind – after we get through this next part of the trail, the hike is almost finished."

"A difficult part of the trail? Mindy said. "Are you serious? I thought the past several miles were pretty unbelievable."

Mike stopped and turned completely around to face the group.

"That sound you hear is the roll of the river and the massive waterfalls ahead of us."

A short distance later they came to a clearing in the trail where the trees seemed to spread apart and the trail widen. The spray from the water gushing over the side of the mountain was incredible, causing a spray of water to spread across the trail. The single line of hikers suddenly became a huddled group of anxious kids as they viewed the waterfalls and river below.

"Wow," John said, "This is huge."

"So, what's the game plan Mike?" Caleb said.

"We have to cross under the waterfalls to continue on the trail. You must be very cautious because slipping on a rock or not being careful where you step could have grave consequences."

He turned and looked at the concerned expressions on their faces and continued, "This is where you'll need to trust me. I've done this a thousand times. I know the way, and I will take you, one by one, across to the other side of the path. What do you think? Is everyone 'ok' with that?"

John said, "Yes, we trust you."

They came to the edge of the trail that seemed to disappear behind the waterfalls. Because of the thick mist, it was very difficult to see where they should step.

"This is where the path continues," Mike said, "So who will go first?"

There was a moment of silence. No one said anything.

Then Caleb spoke up, "I'll go. Hey, what's the alternative, to go back? I don't think so. We're almost finished with this hike. I'm not going back. I trust Mikc knows what he's doing, and I want to be victorious, not defeated by turning back. Besides, isn't this called Victory Trail?"

"Good thinking, Caleb," Mike said as he held out his hand to Caleb.

Caleb gripped Mike's hand, and, in a moment, they disappeared into the waterfalls. The other kids stood by watching in silence, straining to hear anything that might be developing in the unseen area cloaked by rushing water. In what seemed to be eternity, but only several minutes, Mike reappeared.

"One safely on the other side, so who's next?"

"I think I'll go next," Abby said. "I trust you, Mike. Besides what's the point in putting this off? It's too much of a struggle to keep putting something off I know I must do. It makes my stomach hurt." She took Mike's hand and they were gone.

While they were gone, Mindy began taking deep breaths of air, swinging her arms like a bird ready to take flight.

"Ok, guys, I'm going next. Getting through the waterfalls has to be better than all the anxiety of waiting on this side," she said.

Once again, Mike reappeared to Mindy, ready and waiting to take his hand.

"Good for you, Mindy," he said as they disappeared behind the falls.

GOT FAITH?

Those who remained were John, Silas, Kelly and Kathryn. All the time Mike lead the other kids through the falls, Kathryn was very quiet. Finally, in a sudden move that surprised everyone, she moved backward toward the huge mountain wall and pressed her back against its smooth massive rock. The look of fear on her face was painfully clear.

"Kathryn, what's wrong?" Kelly said as she rushed over to where she was standing. "Are you OK?'

Kathryn looked straight ahead, not saying a word as Mike reappeared from delivering his last hiker.

"I think she might be sick," Silas said as Mike walked over to her.

He spoke firmly but with a gentle tone, "Kathryn . . . Kathryn."

Suddenly Kathryn began to cry, her body shaking as she slid her back down the side of the rock until she was sitting on the ground, knees to her chest with her chin resting on them.

"I can't do this! I can't do this!" she sobbed.

Mike crouched down in front of her and tenderly raised her chin with his index finger so that he could look her straight in the eyes. Her eyes were filled with tears that overflowed and ran down her cheeks.

In a sweet and soft voice, he said. "Kathryn, I know you can't do this, I never said you could. But I can, and I said I would do this. I will get you through the falls. You need to trust me."

He raised himself to his feet and said to the others, "Let's let Kathryn settle down while I tell you a story that might help your anxious feelings."

The others quietly leaned back against the mountainside in silence.

"In the summer of 1859 a tightrope walker by the name of Charles Blondin stretched a tightrope over a quarter of a mile across a stretch of Niagara Falls. The thundering sound of rushing water drowned out all other sounds. Huge crowds watched as Charles stepped out on the rope to walk across. He walked 160 feet above the falls going back and forth several times between Canada and the United States. Everyone watched in shock and awe. Once he crossed in a sack, once on stilts, and once on a bicycle. He had proven he could do it. There was no doubt about it.

"Then one day he walked backwards across the tightrope to Canada and returned pushing a wheelbarrow. The story is told that after returning with the wheelbarrow, he asked for some audience participation. He questioned everyone there, 'Do you believe I can carry a person across the falls in this wheelbarrow?' The crowd cheered and shouted 'yes.' It was then that Blondin asked, 'Then, who will get in the wheelbarrow?' Of course, no one did."

Mike looked at the kids and asked, "So what do you think this story is about?"

Silas immediately spoke up, "Faith."

"That's right, Silas. Faith is having confidence in and dependence on someone. You believe what they say, and you will stake your life on it."

"They believed he could do it because they had seen him successfully walk the rope many times," John said.

"Yeah, but it is one thing to watch and another thing to participate," Kelly said.

"That's exactly right, Kelly," Mike said. "It's much like what we are faced with today. When we approached the waterfalls, I mentioned that it was going to be a challenge to get through. I said that you didn't need to worry because I had done this many times, and I would make sure all of you got across safely. Everyone was quick to agree that I would do that for you. You believed I could do it.

"Now is the time to put your belief into action. You don't show you trust me until you step out, and put your hand in mine. That's called faith, trusting that I will do what I promised to do. Not acting is no faith at all."

Kathryn stood up, wiped the tears from her eyes and with a meek smile said, "I'm ready. I know you will get me across the falls safely, I trust you."

Mike came over and put his arm around Kathryn. "Good girl, let's go."

"Way to go, Kathryn," Silas said.

KATHRYN

Mike held Kathryn's hand as they approached the trail that went behind the falls. The mist was so thick it was as though they were stepping through an imaginary magical curtain into another dimension. Once they entered the trail behind the waterfalls, the temperature dropped 20 degrees and the air was heavy and damp. The mist disappeared and the sun that once pierced through the tree-lined path was now cut off by the massive flow of water pouring over the rocks. The path became dark and scary. The roar of the water was deafening. Kathryn squeezed Mike's hand. She was determined to never let go. He stopped and leaned in close to Kathryn to speak to her.

"I will lead you through this path. Hold tight to my hand," he said speaking as loudly as he could so she could hear him over the roar of the water.

"You don't have to worry about that," she thought.

"It's wet and slippery so walk carefully behind me. We will come to a place just up ahead where the path divides. It will seem very logical to you to take the path on the left but please remember that *I know the way.* Just follow me. You will need to trust me."

Kathryn shook her head to affirm his instructions were understood, but said nothing. The two hikers continued the path, carefully choosing each step. As Kathryn watched, Mike carefully navigated through the fallen rocks and moss-covered mountainside. She began to feel a calm spirit come over her. She wasn't afraid anymore because seeing Mike in action had caused her to realize he knew what he was doing, and he was committed to taking care of her. She took a deep breath and smiled.

Her smile quickly disappeared as she looked ahead to see the two paths Mike had told her about. The path to the left was wider than the one on the right. The water flowing over the rocks had thinned out causing the sun to shine through. But the best thing of all was that she could see Abby, Mindy and Caleb standing a short distance away. They were waving their hands and cheering for her.

"Oh, I'm almost there," she said to herself.

"Let's go this way, Mike. I see the others!" she exclaimed.

As quickly as the words came out of her mouth, she was jerked back into reality as Mike pulled her to the right. "Not that way, Missy! We're going this way."

He was pointing to the narrow, dark path to the right that seemed to be heading back into the belly of the mountain and directly opposite to where her friends were waiting for her.

"What?" she yelled.

He stopped and turned to look at her. "Do you remember what I said about the paths when we started through here?"

"Yes, but I saw the other kids that way," she said with an air of frustration. "Didn't you see them?"

"Yes, I did, but believe me when I say 'this is the way' because I can guarantee you do not want to take the other path. Cheer up, we are almost there."

Frustrated, she quit resisting and resigned herself to follow him. They continued the path to the right. It quickly narrowed to the point where it was completely dark. They had to turn sideways to squeeze through the rocks. They slid their feet across the smooth stones in the path. Their clothes got wet and dirty as they rubbed up against the mountain with its cold damp rock and moss. Kathryn's heart was pounding. She could hardly breathe. She held tightly to Mike's hand. He never let go.

As they made their way through the tight space, suddenly a warm breeze hit their faces. Light began to stream into the narrow path. The air seemed lighter and drier and the roar of the waterfalls seemed far away.

"Are we almost there?"

"We're here!" He said as his next few steps ushered them out from behind the falls where Abby, Mindy and Caleb were waiting.

A big smile spread across Kathryn's face. "Whew! That was about the most stressful experience I've ever had," she said. "I don't know what I would have done without you."

Mike just smiled. He took Kathryn by the hand and started walking.

"Remember the path under the falls that went to the left? For all intents and purposes, it seemed like the logical path to take to get to your friends, right?"

"Yes, I remember. I wanted to go that way and I was a little upset that you wouldn't go there."

"I want to show you something," he said.

He took her to the clearing where her friends had been standing earlier. As she stood and looked at the waterfalls from the that side, she discovered it looked quite different. Much to her amazement and awe, she saw that the path she wanted to take ended. It dropped off into a deep ravine, covered with thick vegetation and rock. She realized that when she was standing under the falls wanting to take the path to the left, that she didn't know what was ahead. She couldn't see the danger. She couldn't see that the water flowing over the mountain disguised the danger ahead. The path ended and the deep ravine waited for mistaken hikers. She recognized that the outcome would not have been good. Her perspective looked much different on this side of the falls. It seemed so logical to go that way, especially when she saw her friends just ahead. She recognized that it was only Mike's experience and knowledge of the path that kept her safe. Tears welled up in her eyes as she looked at him and all she could say was, "Thank you. Thank you."

THE CABIN

Meanwhile those who had not yet ventured through the falls, eagerly waited for Mike to reappear. They reflected on what had just unfolded before them.

"Whew, that was intense. I've never seen Kathryn have a meltdown like that. She usually keeps it all together," John said.

"Well, we all have our breaking points," Kelly said. "And if you boys don't mind, I think I will go next because this waiting is about to push me to my breaking point."

"Sure, go ahead. I don't think I can take another female meltdown," Silas said as John laughed. The laughter helped to break the tension.

Suddenly Mike stood before them ready to take the next hiker. One by one the last three hikers eagerly went with him through the falls to meet everyone waiting on the other side.

There was plenty of conversation as each one relived the waterfalls experience. They were glad to be together again and very thankful to have that part of the trail behind them.

"Let's keep pressing onward." Mike said. "I know another place not too far ahead that I want you to see. It's a beautiful and peaceful place. So, let's go."

Weary in both body and spirit, the hikers lifted their backpacks on their shoulders and started hiking. As they walked along, the conversation ceased and a hush came over them, almost a sacred hush. Each one was processing what had just happened. There lingered a sense of victory over fear and a renewed recognition of what can be accomplished through the power of trust in another person.

Hiking had taken on new meaning, and with every step there was renewed strength. The sun began to cast long shadows on the trail and, combined with the warm breeze made everyone know that it was late afternoon. It seemed only a short distance when the trail leveled off and opened into a grassy area with a small pond located in the middle. The pond had crystal clear water that revealed its rocky bottom below. There were tall grasses and cattails, lily pads with frogs and several kinds of hungry fish eagerly waiting for bugs to land on the water.

On the opposite side of the pond was a small cabin. Mike motioned to the hikers to follow him. As they came to the door of the cabin, Mike opened the door and went inside.

"Come on in," he said. "This cabin is here for hikers to enjoy."

"Great," Mindy said. "I'm a little hungry, and I have a snack left in my backpack that I think I will finish off."

"Yeah, I think that sounds good. I have some snacks left, too," said Abby.

They dug into their backpacks looking for the last ounces of food and water as they gathered around the rustic table located in the middle of the room.

The cabin was tidy and neat. A large stone wood burning fireplace was at one end of the cabin. Two large windows were set into the opposite wall that brought much needed light into the room. Everyone was content to relax and munch on snacks. Mike took the opportunity to ask some questions.

"Have you enjoyed the hike?"

With potato chips sticking out of his mouth, Caleb looked up with a surprised expression. He could say nothing.

Abby said, "Well, I can say it will be a hike I will never forget."

"You can say that again," Silas said.

"Now, come on, guys, it's been exciting and fun. Hasn't it?" Kelly asked.

They slowly shook their heads in agreement as Kathryn cautiously answered, "Sure."

They looked at each other as they broke out into laughter.

Mike continued, "Have you learned anything?"

"I've learned plenty," Mindy said. "I've learned not to turn and run when a bear and her cubs are coming after me." Everyone laughed.

"But seriously," she said, "I've learned how I was born into the family of Adam and how I can be born again into God's family. I learned that sin is an attitude, the root, as you put it. And sins are my actions, what I do, because of sin, or the fruit."

"Very good, Mindy. Anyone else learn anything?"

Caleb said, "I learned that God made a way to restore His life back into us by sending Jesus to pay for our sin, so that we could have a relationship with Him because our sin separated us from God."

"That's right, and when His life is restored into a person, God's plan was that when other people would observe that person's life by the way they walked and talked and the choices they made, they would know what God is like," Silas said.

"I've learned what it's like to have to trust another person for my life," Kathryn said with a smile.

"Oh, but don't forget the fog," Kelly said. "There are three things the fog blows into my life to keep me from seeing straight. One is myself. I'm my own worst enemy. I will choose what I want every time. Left to myself, I can be very selfish. And, then, I am daily bombarded by the world and its values, and what it tries to sell me, and get me to believe. Last, but not least, is Satan. He loves to keep me in a fog. He loves to keep me discouraged and defeated. If that doesn't work, he convinces me to be satisfied with life, to become too busy to want a deep personal friendship with God. He also likes to convince me, that I will need to give up too many things in my life to walk with God."

"Sometimes it's allowing the good things to get in the way of the best things," Abby said.

*WAIT A MINUTE!

"Wait a minute! I have a problem with all of this!" John interrupted. He got up from the place he was sitting at the table and began to pace back and forth across the room.

"I understand what everybody has been saying, but I have been struggling with this one thought, who can show who God is all the time? How can I do that? Although I'm a Christian, I know Jesus, I find myself failing time after time, day after day. I'm so powerless to live the life God describes in His Word. A person would have to be perfect like Jesus to do this, and I'm not perfect!" he said in an exasperated tone.

Everyone got quiet as John sat down again and put his head down on the table. Mike slowly walked over to where John was sitting and put his hand on his shoulder.

"You're right, John. You're not perfect. But once again, there's good news. Just as God did not leave us separated from Him because of our sin, but sent Jesus to restore our relationship with Him, he also gave us the perfect example of how to live this thing called 'the Christian life.' It should be no surprise to you, that the same person who is responsible for restoring our lives, is also the one who shows us how to live our lives. And His name is Jesus."

He began to walk around the room as he expressed his thoughts.

"God's provision for every believer is Jesus Christ. You see, Jesus perfectly represented God the Father. Everything Jesus thought, said, and did revealed God. When people observed the life of Jesus, they observed God, the Father."

He walked over to the stone fireplace and rested his arm on the large wooden mantle that stretched across the massive brick.

"Some might say 'well, no big deal for him, he was God' and while that's true, don't forget that he was also totally man. He said that he could do nothing of himself. Since He was God, why would he keep repeating this?" No one said anything.

"I don't really know," Caleb finally said.

"Here's the key. Jesus became *nothing.* He let go of all the qualities he had that only God has and that you and I do not have. He refused to use them. They are qualities such as having always existed, being all-powerful, being able to be present everywhere, all-knowing, ruler over everything, and never changing. He refused to use any of these apart from the will of His Father. So, all that Jesus thought, and said, and did showed who God His Father was, living in and through Him. God the Father was the one doing the works."

"Why did He choose to do it this way?" Kelly asked.

"So, that He could be an example to show how a person is to live in relationship with God. Jesus showed his disciples, as well as you, and me, when He said that without *Him* we could do *nothing*. You might think once again that the disciples had an advantage over us because they had Jesus present with them, but that's not the case. The disciples had their biggest impact on the world after Jesus returned to heaven, not when He was physically with them."

"So, what's the secret, Mike?" Mindy said.

"It's no secret. It can all be found in the Bible, the recorded words of God. Truly, anyone who wants to know God cannot have any kind of relationship with Him apart from reading and studying the Bible. It's God's words to us. If we don't know what God said, how do we know how he wants us to live?"

"How does it all work?" Kelly said.

"Before Jesus died, He told his disciples that He was going away, but that He would come to them as the risen Lord, to not only be with them but to live *in* them by the Holy Spirit. Why?

To show them, and us, that as He as a man, lived only by His Father in Him, now we, as his people are to live only by *His* resurrected life in us. There are many verses in the Bible that speak of this. One verse says that it's not me living, but Jesus living in me."

"I'm familiar with that verse. We memorized it in our youth group a few years ago. It's Galatians 2:20," Abby said.

"Bet you don't remember it now," Caleb said.

Abby stood up in front of the group and began, *"I have been crucified with Christ and I no longer live, but Christ lives in me. The life I live in the body, I live by faith in the Son of God, who loved me and gave Himself for me."*

The group broke out in applause with Caleb putting his fingers to his mouth and loudly whistling.

"Way to go, Abby," John said.

Mike walked over to the table where everyone was seated. He put both hands firmly on the table and leaned in to look closely at them and said, "So, as Christians, what should our response be?" No one spoke up.

"Simply to let God fulfill His purpose for us by receiving the gift of His son Jesus Christ, living in us by the Holy Spirit to be the source of our life and activity, *all that we are and think and do and say.* How do we do this? By faith, by total dependence on Jesus Christ in us."

He walked to the doorway of the cabin and looked out.

Turning back to them, he said, "That's a lot to think about right now, and I think we have spent enough time here, so let's get going. The day is late, and we need to finish this hike before dark."

The hikers quickly jumped to their feet and followed their trusted leader out the door.

WHO'S COMING WITH ME?

After hiking for what seemed to be several hours, the hot and tired travelers came upon a beautiful stream of crystal clear water that had carved its way down the side of the mountain to rest in a natural pool below.

"Hey, I think we might be at ground level," Silas said.

"Yeah, and that means we are not too far from the end of this trail," Kathryn added.

"I just checked my phone, and I have reception!" squealed Abby"

"You're right," Mike said. "The hike is almost complete."

"Well, if that's the case, I'm in. Whose coming with me?" Caleb said.

"What is he talking about," Mindy said as she watched Caleb proceed to remove his backpack from his shoulders. He took his socks and shoes off and jumped into the middle of the stream, clothes and all.

"This is great," he yelled as he splashed around.

He cupped his hands and filled them with water and proceeded to splash the girls standing nearby. Their screams turned to laughter as one by one they jumped into the water.

"They look like they are having way too much fun," John said to Silas as they joined them.

Mike sat on a large boulder at the side of the stream and smiled as he watched the kids enjoy themselves.

After a while Kelly came out of the water to join him. She laughed as she tried to shake off the water from her clothes.

"I wish I had the ability of dogs to shake off all this excess water."

She took the end of her shirttail and twisted it to squeeze out as much water from her wet clothes as she could.

"When you stop, and think about it, this was kind of stupid. We're going to have to finish the rest of this hike in wet clothes. I guess we can use our extra pair of socks we brought in our backpacks – that's a plus."

"I'll let you in on a little secret," Mike whispered. "The trail ends right around the next bend. No one will even have time to dry out." She laughed as she sat down beside him.

"We've really enjoyed the hike. "It's been one I don't think any of us will forget. It has impacted each one of us differently."

She hesitated a moment then said, "I have so many questions rolling around in my head, like how does Jesus live His life through me day by day? What does faith look like on an everyday basis? I know it's so much more than following a set of rules or trying to do good.

"You know, growing up in church like I did, I remember I heard certain catch phrases or words that I became familiar with and I just accepted that I had a handle on 'this is how you live.' But if I would have taken the time to think through these things, I would have had to admit that I wasn't sure what it all meant. So, at this point, I've become satisfied with my relationship with Jesus and have fooled myself into thinking that this is all there is this side of heaven.

"I'm beginning to think, from what you have been telling me, that I have been missing out on an awesome, more personal relationship with Jesus. And it's been available to me all along."

The other kids began to emerge from the stream and shake the water from their clothes. They noticed Mike and Kelly engaged in a lively discussion.

"What are you guys talking about?" John asked. "Looks like it's an interesting one."

"It is," Mike said, "and one that the rest of you should join in."

They gathered around as he continued.

"If you know you are a child of God, He has chosen you and set you apart for a purpose. God makes no mistakes. If His purpose is to have His life lived out through you, then what He asks of you, He is also willing to produce in you. He knows you are unable to produce what He requires so He gives you His Spirit to live in you."

"Yeah, the old gas tank story," Caleb said.

"That's right." It's the purpose of the Holy Spirit to show Jesus to the person in whom He lives."

"And to show us who we are too," Mindy said as she rolled her eyes.

"Yes, that's not always a fun thing, but He reveals weaknesses and habits and attitudes that go against the character and personality of Jesus. He does this by beginning to change the way we think about Him, ourselves and others. It's an inward overhaul."

"Sort of like what our neighbors did to the house down the street from where I live," Silas said.

"They gutted the entire place and totally changed the inside of the house. It looks awesome now, nothing like it was before."

"Great comparison, Silas. That's exactly what the Holy Spirit wants to do in us. He wants to energize us to be delivered from sin and selfishness and to be effective in every right attitude. His purpose is to correct wrong thoughts and choices. He wants to cleanse us from impure urges and refine our desires. He clears away all the weeds so that the traits and qualities of Jesus can grow, and be developed in us, and worked through us."

"It's like clearing a garden of weeds, so all the beautiful flowers can grow," Abby said. "I love flowers."

"That's right, but his role isn't always weeding or correcting. The positive feature of the Holy Spirit is His desire to produce His fruit in us, which produces all types of good works," Mike said.

"The Holy Spirit forms the life of Jesus in us producing love, and good works though us. It's the changing of our character.

And this cannot occur apart from reading and knowing the Word of God. We need to know, and be familiar with how Jesus lived, to know how we are to live. Remember, I told you that the Bible is God's words to us.

"Well, another role of the Holy Spirit is to take the word of God and teach it to you and me. It teaches us what God's will is, and how to live it. I like to think of it this way; the Spirit of God takes the Word of God, and teaches the child of God."

"So, this is so much more than just living life the way I see it – going to church, trying to do the best I can, being a good person, and helping others when I can. And, of course, if I need help from God, I call on him to help me," John said.

"Wow, when you put it that way, it kind of sounds like doing your own thing, and then using God as a rabbit's foot or a lucky charm if you need him," Silas said.

"God wants so much more for us," Mike said. "He has freely given us everything we need to live godly lives. He actively chases after us because he loves us. We don't need to go searching for Him, like He's hiding from us somewhere. He wants to pour His life into us more than we can imagine. No other god does that. Other gods demand people to work to achieve some requirement set up for them. Some people spend their entire lives chasing after an elusive god that is totally incapable of meeting their needs."

Mike got up, stretched and then looked at the kids. "We've been talking a lot about what the God of the universe has done for us and provided for us. But what about us? What's our part in all of this?"

"Yeah, we're not robots that can be programmed or sightless followers that God forces himself upon," Caleb said.

"Just like you said about people who chase after other gods, there must be something we need to do, right?" Mindy said.

"I guess it's just let Him do it! The old 'let go and let God' philosophy," John said.

"That may be true, but my point from the beginning has been, how?" Kelly asked. "I'm getting a clearer picture of the 'what' . . . of God in us by His Spirit showing Jesus to us, so that we become like Him . . . but I need to know the 'how'. You were discouraged back in the cabin, John, when you said that you couldn't live the life God expects. That the good you try to do you don't do and the

bad stuff keeps coming to the surface. I understand that too. So, if God has given us everything we need in Him to live the life He expects, HOW does it work? What IS our part?"
Mike smiled as he came closer to the group, standing in puddles of water with their wet clothes still dripping.

"When John said 'just let go and let God do it,' he was right. But it's more involved than that. It's wrapped up in one word, *surrender*. You think about that word for a while. It's getting late, and we need to finish our hike."

With Mike's prompting, the hikers put on their shoes, gathered their belongings and followed him up the trail, wet clothes and all.

*SURRENDER

The kids walked single file and said very little to one another. They were tired, hungry, and ready to finish the hike and feel the sense of accomplishment it would bring.

"Surrender, what does that mean?" Abby thought.

"Surrender, what does that look like in my life?" Silas pondered.

They had not traveled far when they walked around a bend in the trail, and, much to their surprise, the trail ended. It opened to a well-manicured field. Mowed grass and beautifully groomed flower beds with brick walkways were in full view of the hikers.

"Hey, I think we might be back to civilization!" Mindy shouted.

"I think you're right," Kathryn said.

By this time the entire group was huddled together.

"Is this the back yard of the lodge?" Mindy said.

"Yes, it is. You have accomplished hiking the entire trail, and I am proud of all of you," Mike said.

"But we haven't finished our discussion yet," Silas said. "You wanted us to think about the word surrender. This hike isn't over until we talk about this!"

The others agreed as they gathered around Mike to hear what he had to say.

"I'm glad you decided you wanted to talk about this. I intentionally didn't say anything about our conversation to see what you would do. Just to see if you wanted to finish our discussion.

"You see, just as I waited to see if you had a desire to hear and understand what surrender is, God waits to see if you want to know, and experience more of Him. He's a gentleman. He will not push or force his way upon you, but is ready, willing, and able to pour his life into you if you are willing. That's where surrender comes in.

"Surrender is the total offering of ourselves, body, soul and spirit to Jesus, to do His will, instead of choosing to do our own will. It is recognizing our helplessness. That we have no power or ability on our own to live the life He has called us to live. It's allowing Him to take possession of us. It is giving up the right to ourselves to Jesus Christ. Surrendering our lives is the highest expression of love and grateful worship we can offer God. It's the greatest way to love God back. We must be willing to say that God is superior in all things, that His will must be our priority and focus. Remember, God absolutely surrendered Himself to you and me when He became a man and died for us that He might be entirely ours."

"Oh, that reminds me of another verse I learned," Abby said.

"It's John 3:16, which says that '*God so loved the world that he gave is only Son that whoever believes in him should not perish but have eternal life.*'"

"Yes, Abby, you're right. God gave himself . . . we give ourselves. It's all motivated by love. He loves us; we love Him back. God wants to totally possess us so that we can totally possess Him. God wants us, not what we have or can do for Him. He wants our heart."

"I can see how being pre-occupied with ourselves, our friends and our culture can really hinder our relationship with Jesus," Kelly said.

"You're right. It's not about how many times a week we go to church, or how many programs we are involved in within the church. It's not how many hours we volunteer, and do charity work. It's not even about singing worship songs together. All these things aren't bad, but if they are a substitute, or take the place of the true surrender of our lives to God . . . in his eyes they mean nothing."

"Maybe this illustration will help," Mike said. "We say 'God must be first,' but God says He must be *only.*"

"We can look at life as a blueberry pie. We slice it up, many times unequally, into several pieces. Generally, our thinking is that we give God the biggest slice, and we're satisfied with that. But many times, He gets the smallest slice. Another piece is for home, another for school, another for friends, and so on. We serve up one piece of the pie, we eat it and are totally absorbed in whatever the label is on that piece of pie. Then we take another slice, and whatever that piece is labeled, we devour it. It takes all our time and energy. So, we are shifting through life, living in whatever piece of pie we have cut from the entire pie called 'our life.'

"God says, 'I can't be divided into one slice of your life. If you want to experience me and enjoy my power and presence in everyday life, I must be the filling in the pie that keeps your life together. Whenever you take a slice of pie, no matter what you have labeled it – whether it's school, church, sports, your job, or hanging out with friends, I'm in the middle of it all.' So, no matter what slice of the pie you are involved in, your attitude – words, thoughts, desires, and actions, do not change. Your life doesn't change with every slice of pie. And the awesome thing about living that way, is those around you will be able to recognize the God who lives within you. That's a picture of a surrendered life. So, you must ask yourself, is that your desire? How committed are you to this surrender?

"Let me try to explain it this way; you can choose to live your life like the chicken or the pig. A farmer is getting ready to sit down for breakfast. The farmer's wife is cooking up a ham and egg breakfast for her husband. Both the chicken and the pig are contributors in the development of this breakfast. The chicken is a participant by providing the eggs, but the pig is committed by giving his life."

Caleb said, "So we have a choice to either participate or commit. We can go along and do what seems right to us or what everybody else seems to think is acceptable in a relationship with

God, or we can do what God sees as acceptable, and give our lives fully to Him to allow him to change us and use us, according to His desire and His purposes."

"It's really a win-win situation. We give our lives to God and He gives His life to us," Abby said.

"I think we get the better end of the deal," John said with a smile.

Mike came around the small circle of kids and put his arm around Kathryn. "Several of you made the comment that you didn't know how all this works. Well, the driving force of surrender is *faith.* Faith is the confidence in, and dependence on God. It's believing that He is all that He said He is, and will do all that He said He will do. You would never surrender yourself to someone you didn't trust. Faith is an action word. It's acting on what you believe. It's trusting God is faithful and true to His word. Kathryn, you learned a little about faith on this hike, didn't you?"

Kathryn looked at him with a smile and said, "I sure did. When I was so afraid to go under the waterfalls, I had to depend on you, that you knew what you were doing, that you had been there before and you knew the way. I also had to trust that you cared enough about my safety to see that I got through the waterfalls in one piece. I will never forget that experience, and it will help me to understand surrender."

Mike turned to the rest of the kids and said, "We must recognize that we are helpless to live life on our own. It's not that we have done anything to become helpless, God created us that way, so that we would depend on Him. The key is recognizing and accepting our helplessness. If we never accept our total helplessness apart from Him, we will stay struggling in the fog and never experience the full working of God in us.

"He knows our weaknesses and our struggles. He knows how helpless we are. Even in our surrender, He is right there to accomplish in us the desire of our willing hearts. Surrender takes us from self-centeredness to God-centeredness. It truly is a partnership. It's a life-long growth process. It is the life of Jesus working in us as we live moment by moment in obedient partnership with Him. He lives in us by His Spirit, so that, as we are surrendered to Him, we can walk through every day and every situation in His power.

"We do not have to give in to selfish desires, but can be so in love with Jesus and committed to Him that His life and character will change us and be seen in us. There is no better way to live life. It's a life full of meaning and purpose, of joy and fulfillment, of power and victory. This is called the Christ life."

"Hey, and that's God's divine design for mankind!" Silas shouted.

WHAT AM I DOING HERE?

"John . . . John! . . . Can you hear me?" John's father excitedly said. "I think he might be waking up. I think he's opening his eyes!"

John tried to open his eyes, but all was blurred. His head was pounding with every beat of his heart. "Where am I?" he said in a slow groggy voice.

"You're in the hospital, honey."

"What am I doing here?"

John's mom pampered him by adjusting his pillow and straightening his covers.

She asked, "Would you like your head raised a bit, son?"

"Yes, but please, tell me, what happened?"

His mom leaned in to kiss the side of his cheek and said, "We were so worried about you. We have been here day and night since the accident."

"Since the accident? What are you talking about?"

Mr. Riley summoned the nurse who quickly came to John's side to take his vitals.

"He seems to be responding well. I think the worst is over. I will let the doctor know," she said as she left the room.

"Wait! Mom, Dad. I have to tell you about our hiking trip," he said as he began to think more clearly. "It was the best experience I ever had. Wow! All the things that happened . . . I don't know where to begin . . . the bears . . . the fog . . . the waterfalls. And Mike! What a guy. He was the best. We just loved to hear all he had to tell us."

Mr. and Mrs. Riley stood speechless in the middle of the hospital room. Neither of them knew what to say.

John looked at his parents. "What? Why are you looking at me that way?" He knew something wasn't right. He looked around the room.

"Where are the others? I'm sure they have a lot to tell too. He paused for a moment, then said, "Ok, tell me what is going on. What happened? How did I end up here?"

Mr. Riley came to John's bedside and said, "Well, son, you had a terrible fall. You slipped off the side of a steep embankment and rolled several hundred feet through trees, rocks and thick vegetation. You have some bruises and cuts. But the worst injury was to your head. Your head hit a rock on the way down and knocked you out. You have been in a coma for a week. We have been so worried about you."

"Wait a minute! Wait a minute! A week?" John exclaimed.

"Are you telling me we never finished the hike?"

"Yes, honey. Your group hadn't gone very far before all of this happened," Mrs. Riley said.

"And Mr. Jensen and your friends were a tremendous help in your rescue. You had to be airlifted out of there. They have been very worried about you. Sam Bennet and the entire youth group have been meeting together every day to pray for your recovery."

John sat straight up in his bed adjusting his covers. "So, that's why Mr. Jensen left," he mumbled. "It wasn't another group that had an emergency. It was because of me!"

He looked directly at his parents and said, "Ok, where's Mike. I know he will be able to explain all of this. I just talked to him."

John's father responded with a blank look on his face, "Who's Mike, son?"

"Our guide, dad!" John said excitedly.

Mrs. Riley had a worried look on her face and said "Honey, don't you remember that Mr. Jensen, Silas's dad, was your guide?"

John sat quietly deep in thought for a long time.

Finally, he said, "Yes, he was at the beginning of the hike. But then he was gone. Right now, I don't remember any other guide but Mike."

"Ok," Mr. Riley said. "You'd better rest for now. I'm sure after you talk with your friends, everything will become clearer."

Later that evening, the night nurse pestered him to get up and start moving, which at first exhausted him. But he was glad to be able to put one foot in front of the other as he took short walks down the hall, so he didn't complain. The night exercise made him feel better and ready to tackle the next day. In his mind 'the next day' meant finding out what happened on the hike from those who were there – his friends.

That night when everyone was gone and the halls were quiet, John couldn't sleep. He continued deep in thought all night, tossing and turning in his bed.

"I don't understand this. It all seemed so real . . . it has to be real," he thought as he finally faded into sleep.

REALITY

The morning sun shone brightly through the hospital windows as John opened his eyes to another day. His headache was gone, and he even had an appetite. He sat up in bed enjoying his breakfast. "I thought everybody hated hospital food. This isn't that bad," he mumbled to himself as he chowed down.

"I'm so ready to talk to Caleb and Silas and the girls," he thought to himself. "They will certainly know Mike, and the crazy adventure we experienced."

After breakfast was over, he heard laughter and loud chatter outside in the hall, which made him know his friends were on their way to his room. He sat up straight in his bed ready for their entrance. The girls entered the room first, carrying flowers and a big box of candy.

"These are for you, John," Abby said. "We're so glad you're all right."

"Yeah, you had us worried," Kelly said.

"We were so glad to get the phone call from your parents last night. You are definitely an answer to prayer," Silas said.

"Hey man, glad to see you with your eyes open today," Caleb joked. "I thought you just might decide to stay in la la land."

John looked around at all his friends. "I'm so excited you guys are here. Wasn't that the craziest, most exciting hiking trip?"

"What? You mean the hike that never happened?" Silas asked as everyone broke into laughter.

John squirmed in his bed. "Never happened? You're not going to give me the same line my parents did, are you? They told me the accident happened at the beginning of the hike up Victory Trail, and we never got to finish."

"They told you the truth, John," Kathryn said as she came close to his bed. "And it was called Scenic Trail, not Victory Trail."

John thought about that for a minute and then said, "What about Mike, you guys? You do remember him, don't you? Nobody could forget him."

"Who's Mike?" Kelly asked.

As she looked at John's face, she sensed he was struggling to make sense of everything. She wanted to be sensitive.

"Obviously, you have experienced something we didn't, John."

"Tell us what happened to you?" Abby said.

"I remember a man standing over me as I lay on the ground. I didn't think about why I was there. I just remember how pleasant he was. He held out his hand to me and asked if he could help me up. I took his hand, and he said his name was Mike, that he was a guide on the mountain. Before I knew it, we were walking on the trail, all of us, and Mike was our guide. He was an amazing man. He taught us so much about Jesus and truth and life, more than I had ever heard or known before. I just can't believe none of you remember him."

For a few minutes, the room was silent. The kids looked at one another as it became very clear that while John was in a coma, he had experienced some amazing things.

Mindy finally spoke up, "Wow, that must have been some trip you were on, John. It sounds like it could have been an out-of-body experience. It would've been nice to have hiked with you, but unfortunately, that didn't happen. And due to your showing off and messing around on the trail, you caused all of us to forfeit the trip. I'm glad you're ok, believe me when I say that. But do you know how hard I worked to raise money to go on this trip? You have no idea the hours I spent babysitting, helping around the house and doing odd jobs for people, just to make sure I could go this summer. And all you can say is you had this awesome hiking experience, while we spent the last week worried about you. Sorry, it just might take me a little while to join in your excitement."

"I'm so sorry about that, Mindy. Really, I am. If I could change things I would. But believe me, you were all there, and some unbelievable things happened to all of us. Maybe I can share a little of what happened.

"Caleb . . . you my man, were spiritually dead when you started this hike, but by the end of the hike, you were born into the family of God."

"What? I don't understand," Caleb said.

"Oh, we are going to spend some serious time together, my friend," John said.

"And what about you, Abby? Have you and Mindy been chased by any bears lately?"

They looked at each other in surprise. Abby said, "I think you really bumped your head John. We didn't get far enough into the woods to even begin to see a bear."

"Silas, buddy. You kept everyone on track. You were our information center. And Kelly, you were so full of questions, good questions for Mike, and he answered them all!"

John swung his legs over the side of the bed and in one fluid motion was on his feet. He walked across the room, shaking his finger at Kathryn.

"Ok . . . Ok, then how about you Kathryn?" Talk about tense moments. You had the famous waterfalls experience. That about put everyone over the edge."

Kathryn looked at him with concern, wanting to be sympathetic, but said, "Ok, John, whatever you say."

John stood motionless staring at her for a moment and then said, "Oh! We have to talk!"

The kids stood in silence around John. He knew by the look on each face what he must do. He knew he had to deal with reality. And the reality was, that he was the only one who had been on this hike. Like a lightbulb that is turned on in a dark room, John suddenly realized that what he had experienced, was a personal, one-of-a-kind, adventure from God.

"Why him? Why did God choose him to experience this?" he thought.

He didn't say anything for quite some time. The room was unusually quiet. Everyone was hanging on, just waiting for his next words.

Finally, he broke the silence. "Well, all I know, is my life will never be the same. I will not live my life in the same way I did before the accident. I have been changed."

"I'm a little suspicious of all this, man," Caleb said. "How could bumping your head, and being in a coma for a week, change your entire life?" I don't know if I buy into all this God adventure stuff you're telling us about." But you are my good friend and I know you wouldn't just make this stuff up on purpose. I'm just glad to have my friend back. So, hurry up and get well so we can have a B Ball pick-up game at my house, ok?"

"I don't know what to say, and yet, I have so much to say. I don't know where to start," John said. "Listen, we're all trying to figure out what life is about. We're just kids. So, wouldn't you like to know that your life had a special purpose? Wouldn't you like to know what it's like to *really* be loved by someone? How about being accepted . . . totally and completely, arms open wide, come on in, received by someone – no strings attached? There's nothing you must do or say. No club to join. Just come as you are.

"We're trying to figure out our future and what it's going to look like. We're trying to decide what we believe about our culture, and the ever-changing values society throws at us. We're trying to figure it all out! Wouldn't it be great to know that someone has already done all this for us, and all we need to do is let Him guide us?

"I now know my life has purpose and meaning. I'm not just here to hang out. I have seen faith in action, that is, trusting another person for my life. I have learned to be on guard, to not live in fear, to have victory over Satan's lies. I've learned that life isn't all about me, that selfishness is a deal breaker. That giving God control of my life, and letting Jesus live through me, is the best way to live.

"I've come to know, *really* know Jesus in a more personal and powerful way. I'm beginning to see through different eyes. I am beginning to see how God is changing my thinking because He has changed my heart. I'm beginning to see new things all the time.

"Let me give you an example. The hospital brought me my breakfast this morning. It was pancakes. I looked at the pancakes, and suddenly, things made sense. Pancakes consist of batter, milk and eggs; three different ingredients, right? And yet, they're not pancakes until all the ingredients are blended together, put on the griddle, and flipped. The finished pancakes end up looking completely different from the original ingredients. Yeah, yum, now they can be eaten. That's their original purpose."

John started to pace back and forth across the room.

"You see, there's Jesus, the Holy Spirit and me." He clasped his fingers together to show the connection.

"The Holy Spirit takes the life of Jesus, with all His qualities and brings Him alive in me. When my surrendered life – he's in control, not me," he said with a grin, "is blended with Jesus and the Holy Spirit, I begin to look different. But I'm not done yet. Because it's the flipping on the griddle that holds everything together. The griddle is the Word of God, the Bible. If the pancake never gets to the griddle, it just sits in the bowl, never becoming what it is supposed to be.

"If I'm not in the Word of God, my manual for life, I'll never be what I'm supposed to be, the completed work of God. But when all the ingredients are blended and working together, my life is what it was created to be. My actions and attitudes become the actions and attitudes of Jesus. Everything I say and do will reflect the Lord Jesus. Now, when someone sees my life in action, they can see what Jesus is like."

He paused, then looked around at everyone.

"You asked, 'Who's Mike?' Well, he was my guide. He was the one who taught me about these things. And he taught you guys too . . . that is, when I was in my coma. I wish you could have been there, I really do. Then you would be feeling the same things I'm feeling. Wow! The conversations we could be having!"

Caleb walked over and put his hand on John's shoulder. "Dude, I believe you did experience something. It's obvious. But I'm not sure about all this. I need to think about it."

"Well, I definitely want to hear more," Kelly said.

John looked at them and said, "I do know this – I can't keep to myself what God showed me on this hike. It's too important. It's life changing, and I want to share it with all of you."

"Ok, John, maybe you can be our guide, like Mike," Kathryn said with a smile.

"Maybe I can," John said.

He slowly returned to his bed, laid his head back on his pillow and stared at the ceiling. Suddenly a big smile broke out across his face as he shouted, "Wow! This has been an awesome adventure!"

SCRIPTURE VERSES

Chapter Scripture Verses

(The italic words in parenthesis are personally added for clarity)

**WHY ARE YOU HERE?*

Genesis 1:1-2 – In the beginning God created the heavens and the earth. Now the earth was formless and empty, darkness was over the surface of the deep, and the Spirit of God was hovering over the waters.

Genesis 1:26 & 27 – God said, "Let us *(Father, Son and Holy Spirit)* make man in our image, in our likeness *(resemblance, not physical but in moral character and attitude)"* . . . So, God created man in His own image *(copy)*, in the image of God He created him; male and female, He created them.

Genesis 2:7 – The Lord God formed man from the dust of the ground and breathed *(Spirit)* into his nostrils the breath of God *(life of God)*, and man became a living soul *(physical and spiritual life)*.

Romans 11:36 – For from Him and through Him and to Him are all things – For all things originate with Him and come from Him; all things live through Him, and all things center in and tend to consummate and to end in Him. To Him be glory forever! Amen – so be it.

Colossians 1:15-17 – He *(Jesus)* is the image of the invisible God, the firstborn over all creation. For by Him all things were created: things in heaven and on earth, visible and invisible, whether thrones or powers or rulers or authorities; all things were created by Him and for Him. He is before all things, and in Him all things hold together.

**THE GARDEN*

Genesis 3:1 – Now the serpent was more subtle and crafty than any living creature of the field which the Lord God had made. And he *(Satan)* said to the woman, "Can it really be that God has said, 'You shall not eat of every tree of the garden?' *(casting doubt)*.

Genesis 3:4 -5 – But the serpent said, "You shall not surely die. For God knows that in the day you eat of it your eyes will be opened, and you will be as God, knowing the difference between good and evil, and blessing and calamity." *(lie)*.

Genesis 3:6 – And when the woman saw *(considered, thought about, more than a look)* that the tree was good (suitable and pleasant) for food *(lust of the flesh)*, and it was delightful to look at *(lust of the eyes)* and a tree to be desired to make one wise *(pride of life),* she took of its fruit and ate; and she gave some also to her husband, and he ate.

*DEAD OR ALIVE

What God Said

Genesis 3:16-17, 19 – To the woman He said, "I will greatly multiply your pain in childbirth, in pain you shall bring forth children; yet your desire shall be for your husband, and he shall rule over you."
Then to Adam He said, "Because you have listened to the voice of your wife, and have eaten from the tree about which I have commanded you, saying, 'You shall not eat from it.' Cursed is the ground because of you. In toil, you shall eat of it all the days of your life.
By the sweat of your face you shall eat bread, till you return to the ground, because from it you were taken; for you are dust, and to dust you shall return."

Result of Disobedience – Sin

Romans 6:23 – For the wages *(payment)* of sin is death . . .

Romans 3:23 – For all have sinned and fall short of the glory of God *(spiritual separation from God, unable to express His character and likeness).*

Romans 5:12 – Therefore, as sin came into the world through one man *(Adam),* and death as the result of sin, so death spread to all men, (no one being able to stop it *or* to escape its power) because all men sinned.

Spiritually Dead – Separated from the Life of God

Ephesians 2:1-2 – As for you, you were dead in your transgressions *(misbehaviors)* and sins, in which you used to live when you followed the ways of this world and of the ruler of the kingdom of the air *(Satan),* the spirit who is now at work in those who are disobedient.

Ephesians 4:17-19 – So I tell you this, and insist on it in the Lord, that you must no longer live as the Gentiles *(heathen)* do, in the futility *(senselessness)* of their thinking. They are darkened in their understanding and separated from the life of God because of the ignorance that is in them due to the hardening of their hearts. Having lost all sensitivity, they have given themselves over to sensuality so as to indulge in every kind of impurity, with a continual lust for more.

Restoration of Life through Jesus

1Corinthians 15:22 – For as in Adam all die, so in Christ all will be made alive.

Ephesians 2: 4-5 – But because of His great love for us, God, who is rich in mercy, made us alive with Christ even when we were dead in transgressions – it is by grace you have been saved.

Romans 5:19 – For just as through the disobedience of the one man *(Adam)* the many were made sinners, so also through the obedience of the one man *(Jesus)* the many will be made righteous.

Romans 5:6,8 – You see, at just the right time, when we were still powerless, Christ died for the ungodly.
But God demonstrates His own love for us in this: While we were still sinners, Christ died for us.

John 3:3 – Jesus answered him, I assure you, most solemnly I tell you, that unless a person is born again (anew, from above), he cannot ever see – know, be acquainted with (and experience) – the kingdom of God.

John 3:5-7 – Jesus answered, I assure you, most solemnly I tell you, except a man be born of water and (even) the Spirit, he cannot (ever) enter the kingdom of God. What is born of (from) the flesh is flesh – of the physical is physical; and what is born of the Spirit is spirit. Marvel not – do not be surprised, astonished – at My telling you, you must all be born anew (from above).

John 1:12 – But to as many as did receive and welcome Him *(Jesus)*, He gave the authority (power, privilege, right) to become the children of God, that is, to those who believe in – adhere to, trust in and rely on – His *(Jesus)* name.

1John 3:1 – How great is the love the Father has lavished on us, that we should be called the children of God! And that is what we are! The reason the world does not know us is that it did not know Him.

1Peter 1:23 – Having been born again, not of corruptible seed but incorruptible, through the word of God which lives and abides forever.

**FOG . . . FOG . . . FOG*

Sin, The Root – What I Am

Psalms 51:5 – Surely I was sinful at birth, sinful from the time my mother conceived me.

Matthew 15:18 – But the things that come out of the mouth come from the heart, and these make a man unclean.

Romans 7:19-21 – For what I do is not the good I want to do; no, the evil I do not want to do – this I keep on doing. Now if I do what I do not want to do, it is no longer I who do it, but it is sin living in me that does it. So, I find this law at work: When I want to do good, evil is right there with me.

Romans 8:7,8 – The mind set on the flesh is hostile towards God; for it does not subject itself to the law of God, for it is not even able *to do so;* and those who are in the flesh cannot please God.

Sins, The Fruit – What I Do

Psalms 58:3 – Even from birth the wicked go astray; from the womb, they are wayward and speak lies.

Galatians 5:17 – For the sinful nature desires what is contrary to the Spirit, and the Spirit what is contrary to the sinful nature. They are in conflict with each other, so that you do not do what you want.

Jesus, the Remedy for Sin/Sins

Romans 6:6-7 – Our old sinful selves were crucified with Christ so that sin might lose its power in our lives. We are no longer slaves to sin. For when we died with Christ, we were set free from the power of sin.

1Corinthians 15:3 – For I passed on to you, first of all what I also had received, that Christ, the Messiah, the Anointed One, died for our sins in accordance with (what) the Scriptures (foretold).

***DON'T BLOW IT OFF**

Selfishness

James 3:14-16 – But if you have bitter jealousy and selfish ambition in your heart, do not be arrogant and *so* lie against the truth. This wisdom is not that which comes down from above, but is earthly, natural, demonic. For where jealousy and self-ambition exist, there is disorder and every evil thing.

Philippians 2:3 – Do nothing out of selfish ambition or vain conceit, but in humility consider others better than yourselves.

Psalms 119:36 – Turn my heart toward your statutes and not toward selfish gain.

Titus 2:11-12 – For the grace of God that brings salvation has appeared to all men. It teaches us to say "No" to ungodliness and worldly passions, and to live self-controlled, upright and godly lives in this present age.

World Culture

1Corinthians 3:19-20 – For this world's wisdom is foolishness – absurdity and stupidity – with God. For it is written, He lays hold of the wise in their (own) craftiness; And again, The Lord knows the thoughts *and* reasoning of the (humanly) wise and recognizes how futile they are.

James 4:4 – You (are like) unfaithful wives (having illicit love affairs with the world) *and* breaking your marriage vow to God! Do you not know that being the world's friend is being God's enemy? So, whoever chooses to be a friend of the world takes his stand as an enemy of God.

1John 2:15-17 – Do not love the world or anything in the world. If anyone loves the world, the love of the Father is not in him. For everything in the world – the cravings of sinful man, the lust of his eyes, and the boasting of what he has and does – comes not from the Father but from the world. The world and its desires pass away, but the man who does the will of God lives forever.

Romans 12:2 – Do not conform any longer to the pattern of this world *(don't let the world press you into its mold)* but be transformed by the renewing of your mind. Then you will be able to test and approve what God's will is – His good, pleasing and perfect will.

Satan

Roaring Lion – 1Peter 5:8 – Be self-controlled and alert. Your enemy the devil prowls around like a roaring lion looking for someone to devour.

Radical Liar – John 8:44 . . . He was a murderer from the beginning, not holding to the truth, for there is no truth in him. When he lies, he speaks his native language, for he is a liar and the father of lies.

Radiant Light – 2Corinthians 3:14 . . . for Satan, himself masquerades as an angel of light.

Satan's Effect on Unbelievers

2Corinthians 4:4 – For the god of this world has blinded the unbelievers' minds (that they should not discern the truth), preventing them from seeing the illuminating light of the Gospel of the glory of Christ, the Messiah, Who is the image *and* likeness of God.

2Thessalonians 2:9-10 – The coming (of the lawlessness one, the Antichrist) is through the activity *and* working of Satan, and will be attended by great power and with all sorts of (pretended) miracles and signs *and* delusive marvels – (all of them) lying wonders – and by unlimited seduction to evil *and* with all wicked deception for those who are (going to perdition,) perishing because they did not welcome the Truth *but* refused to love it that they might be saved.

Satan's Effect on Believers

2Corinthians 11:3 – But I am afraid that just as Eve was deceived by the serpent's cunning, your minds may somehow be led astray from your sincere and pure devotion to Christ.

Ephesians 6:11 – Put on the full armor of God so that you can take your stand against the devil's schemes *(strategies).*

2Corinthians 2:11 – . . . in order that Satan might not outwit us. For we are not unaware of his schemes.

***WAIT A MINUTE!**

John 1:14 – The Word *(Jesus)* became flesh and made His dwelling among us. We have seen His glory, the glory of the One and Only, who came from the Father, full of grace and truth.

John 1:18 – No man has ever seen God at any time; the only unique Son, the only-begotten God, who is in the bosom (that is, in the intimate presence) of the Father, He *(Jesus)* has declared Him *(God)* – He has revealed Him, brought Him out where He can be seen; He has interpreted Him, *and* He has made Him known.

Hebrews 1:3 – The Son is the radiance of God's glory *(character)* and the exact representation of His being sustaining all things by His powerful word. After He had provided purification for sins, He sat down at the right hand of the Majesty in heaven.

Philippians 2:6-7 – Who *(Jesus)*, although being essentially one with God *and* in the form of God (possessing the fullness of the attributes – *or qualities* which make God God), did not think this equality with God was a thing to be eagerly grasped or retained; but stripped Himself (of all privileges and rightful dignity) to assume the form of a servant (slave), in that He became like men *and* was born a human being.

John 5:19 – Jesus gave them this answer, "I tell you the truth, the Son can do nothing by Himself; He can do only what He sees His Father doing, because whatever the Father does, the Son also does."

John 5:30 – By myself I can do nothing; I judge only as I hear, and my judgement is just, for I seek not to please myself but Him who sent me.

John 6:38 – For I have come down from heaven not to do my will, but to do the will of Him who sent me."

John 14:10-11 – Don't you believe that I am in the Father, and the Father is in me? The words I say to you are not just my own. Rather, it is the Father, living in me, who is doing the work. Believe me when I say that I am in the Father and the Father is in me . . .

John 15:4-5 – Remain in Me *(Jesus)*, and I will remain in you. No branch can bear fruit by itself; it must remain in the vine. Neither can you bear fruit unless you remain in Me. I am the vine; you are the branches. If a man remains in Me and I in him, he will bear much fruit; apart from Me you can do nothing.

1John 2:5-6 – . . . If anyone obeys His word, God's love is truly made complete in him. This is how we know we are in Him: Whoever claims to live in Him must walk as Jesus did.

1John 3:24 – Those who obey His commands live in Him, and He in them. And this is how we know that He lives in us: We know it by the Spirit He gave us.

***_WHO'S COMING WITH ME?_**

Spirit

John 14: 16-17 – And I will ask the Father, and He will give you another Comforter (Counselor, Helper, Intercessor, Advocate, Strengthener and Standby) that He may remain with you forever – the Spirit of Truth. The world cannot receive (welcome, take to its heart), because it does not see Him, nor know *and* recognize Him. But you know *and* recognize Him, for He lives with you (constantly) and will be in you.

Romans 8:16 – The Spirit Himself testifies with our spirit that we are God's children.

Galatians 4:6 – Because you are sons, God sent the Spirit of His Son into our hearts, the Spirit who calls out, "*Abba (Daddy)* Father."

1John 4: 13 – We know *(perceive, recognize and understand)* that we live in Him and He in us, because He has given us of His Spirit.

Philippians 1:6 – And I am convinced *and* sure of this very thing, that He Who began a good work in you will continue until the day of Jesus Christ – right up to the time of His return – developing (that good work) *and* perfecting *and* bringing it to full completion in you.

Philippians 2:13 - For it is God working in you, giving you the desire to obey Him and the power to do what pleases Him.

Galatians 5:16 – But I say, walk *and* live habitually in the (Holy) Spirit – responsive to *and* controlled *and* guided by the Spirit; then you will certainly not gratify the cravings *and* desires of the flesh – of human nature without God.

Galatians 5:22-23 – But the fruit of the (Holy) Spirit, (the work which His presence within accomplishes) – is love, joy (gladness), peace, patience (an even temper), kindness, goodness, faithfulness, gentleness (meekness, humility) and self-control (self-restraint). Against such things there is no law (that can bring a charge).

2 Corinthians 3:17-18 – Now the Lord is the Spirit, and where the Spirit of the Lord is, there is freedom. And we, who with unveiled faces all reflect the Lord's glory, are being transformed into His likeness with ever-increasing glory, which comes from the Lord, who is the Spirit.

Word of God

2Timothy 3:16 – All scripture is God-breathed and is useful for teaching, rebuking, correcting and training in righteousness, so that the man of God may be thoroughly equipped for every good work.

Jeremiah 15:16 – When your words came, I ate *(devoured)* them; they were my joy and my heart's delight . . .

Isaiah 55:11 – . . . so is my word that goes out from my mouth: It will not return to Me empty, but will accomplish what I desire and achieve the purpose for which I sent it.

Colossians 3:16 – Let the word (spoken by) the Christ, the Messiah, have its home (in your hearts and minds) *and* dwell in you in (all its) richness.

Hebrews 4:12 – For the word of God is living and active. Sharper than any double-edged sword, it penetrates even dividing soul and spirit, joints and marrow; it judges the thoughts and attitudes of the heart.

Psalms 119:9 – How can a young man keep his way pure? By living according to your word.

Psalms 119:11 – I have hidden your word in my heart that I might not sin against you.

Psalms 119:105 – Your word is a lamp to my feet and a light to my path.

*SURRENDER

1Corinthians 6:19-20 – Do you not know that your body is a temple of the Holy Spirit, who is in you, whom you have received from God? You are not your own; you were bought at a price. Therefore, honor God with your body.

Romans 12:1-2 – I appeal to you therefore, brethren, *and* beg of you in view of (all) the mercies of God, to make a decisive dedication of your bodies – presenting all your members *(physical body parts)* and faculties *(talents and capabilities)* – as a living sacrifice, holy (devoted, consecrated) and well-pleasing to God, which is your reasonable (rational, intelligent) service *and* spiritual worship.
Do not be conformed *(pressed into the mold)* to this world – this age, fashioned after and adapted to its external, superficial customs. But be transformed (changed) by the (entire) renewal of your mind – by its new ideals and its new attitude – so that you may prove (for yourselves) what is the good and acceptable and perfect will of God, *even* the thing which is good and acceptable and perfect (in His sight for you).

Hebrews 11:1 – Now faith is the assurance (the confirmation, the title-deed) of the things (we) hope for, being the proof of things (we) do not see *and* the conviction of their reality – faith perceiving as real fact what is not revealed to the senses.

Hebrews 12:1-3 – Therefore, since we are surrounded by such a great cloud of witnesses, let us throw off everything that hinders and the sin that so easily entangles, and let us run with perseverance the race marked out for us. Let us fix our eyes on Jesus, the author and perfecter of our faith, who for the joy set before Him endured the cross, scorned its shame, and sat down at the right hand of the throne of God.

Acts 17:28 – For in Him we live and move and have our being.

2Peter 1:3-4 – His divine power has given us everything we need for life and godliness through our knowledge of Him who called us by His own glory and goodness. Through these He has given us His very great and precious promises, so that through them you may participate in the divine nature and escape the corruption in the world caused by evil desires.

Philippians 2:13 – For it is God working in you, giving you the desire to obey Him and the power to do what pleases Him.

Galatians 3:3 – Are you so foolish? After beginning with the Spirit, are you now trying to attain your goal by human effort?

1Thessalonians 5:23-24 – And may the God of peace Himself sanctify you through and through – that is, separate you from profane things, make you pure and wholly consecrated to God – and may your spirit and soul and body be preserved sound and complete (and found) blameless *(refers to motives of the mind, heart, ambitions, purposes, speaking and doing)* at the coming of our Lord Jesus Christ, the Messiah. Faithful is He Who is calling you (to Himself) *and* utterly trustworthy, and He will also do it (that is, fulfill His call by hallowing *(blessing)* and keeping you).

2Corinthians 5:17 – Therefore, if anyone is in Christ, he is a new creation; the old is gone and the new has come.

1John 2:5-6 – . . . If anyone obeys His word, God's love is truly made complete in him. This is how we know we are in Him: Whoever claims to live in Him must walk as Jesus did.

Sharon DeBord Chako has a Bachelor's degree in Communication and Biblical Studies. She loves to express herself through words, and believes thoughts written on paper are priceless treasures. She lives with her husband, Larry, and their Schnoodle dog, Franklin, in Bluffton, Ohio.